I froze. Immediately I switched my gaze from Gemma's white, tense face to Mum and Dad. The possibility of our parents splitting up was something I hadn't allowed myself to think about too much because it simply wasn't going to happen. That was what I'd told myself, over and over again. I waited for Mum and Dad to reply – for the denials, the reassurances, the explanations that they were just 'going through a bad patch'...

None of those things came.

For my dad, who took me to my very first football match

www.thebeautifulgamebooks.co.uk

ORCHARD BOOKS
338 Euston Road, London NW1 3BH
Orchard Books Australia
Level 17/207 Kent Street, Sydney, NSW 2000

First published in 2010 by Orchard Books

ISBN 978 1 40830 424 2

A CIP catalogue record for this book is available
from the British Library.

10 9 8 7 6 5 4 3 2 1

Printed in Great Britain

Orchard Books is a division of Hachette Children's Books,
an Hachette UK company.

www.hachette.co.uk

THE BEAUTIFUL GAME

Friends and football – the perfect match

GOLDEN GIRL GRACE

NARINDER DHAMI

ORCHARD BOOKS

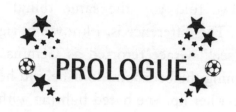

PROLOGUE

"You're being a real idiot, Gemma!" Grace yelled furiously. "You ought to wake up and take a long hard look at yourself!"

Grace didn't lose her temper very often, but when she did, there were fireworks. And these days it always seemed to be her sister Gemma who was responsible for winding her up, Grace thought angrily. Why couldn't she and Gemma just get along like they used to? After all, they were twins, and twins were *supposed* to be close...

"What the hell do you mean?" Gemma shouted, her face pink with rage. "*You're* the one who's making a fool of yourself, and you just won't admit it!"

"Oh, don't start *that* again." Grace pretended to yawn in a bored way, which she knew would *totally* annoy Gemma. "I've told you a million times, you've got it all wrong—"

"And I've told *you* the same thing!" Gemma snapped. "The difference is, I know I'm right!"

"We'll see!" Grace retorted as Gemma flounced off, slamming the bedroom door behind her.

Grace bit her lip. She hated fighting with Gemma like this, but there was no way she was going to back down. The feelings she was experiencing at the moment were brand-new and wonderful, and she wasn't going to give that up for anybody. Not even Gemma.

CHAPTER ONE

I was surrounded, with nowhere to go. There were three defenders hassling me for the ball and preventing me from passing to Hannah or Lauren, both of whom I could see hovering hopefully around me in the penalty area. There was no way I could take a shot, either, because I had my back to the goal.

Or was there?

My dad's voice popped into my head.

When you think there's nothing you can do, go for the unexpected...

Fine. So instead of trying to pass the ball to

Hannah or Lauren or any of my other Stars team-mates, instead of trying to turn and get a shot in – I backheeled the ball as hard as I could in the direction of Melfield United's goal.

I'd seen a couple of Premier League players score like that, but I never *dreamt* I'd be able to do the same. Because I was kicking the ball backwards, I couldn't hit it with very much force. However, I was in luck because my unusual shot took the Melfield goalie completely by surprise. I spun round just in time to see the ball roll into the far corner of the net.

There was a gasp of surprise from the parents grouped around the touchline, and they all broke into applause. I blushed. Even though I totally *love* scoring goals, I always get a bit embarrassed when I'm the centre of attention.

"Grace, aren't you just the *coolest* striker in the whole league!" Lauren shrieked joyfully, rushing over to leap on my back. Luckily, Lauren is tiny and petite, or she might have sent me flying!

"Grace, how fab are you?" Jasmin squealed. She bounded over, her black ponytail bobbing crazily, and threw her arms around me (and Lauren, who was still clinging to me).

"Going for the hat-trick, are we, Grace?" Hannah

wanted to know, smiling hugely. I grinned back at her. I'd already scored a goal in the first half, although it hadn't been as spectacular as this one. There'd been a scramble in the Melfield goalmouth, and, in the ruck, I'd just managed to get my toe to the ball. With the goalie wrong-footed, it had rolled across the line agonisingly slowly. But anyway, as my dad always says: *it doesn't matter how you score – as long as you score!*

"Maybe," I replied with a wink.

I glanced down the field at Georgie, our goalie, and Katy, our centre-back. I'd heard Georgie whooping and cheering when I scored – she's never shy about showing her feelings! Now she and Katy both waved at me, and Georgie pointed both of her index fingers at the sky. I knew exactly what she meant. *We're on our way up to the top league!* We were all dying to win promotion this year, and we were second in the table at the moment. It was only October, though, so there was still ages to go.

"Good work, Grace," called our new coach, Ria Jones, who was standing watching the game with our parents.

As we hurried back to our positions for kick-off, I caught sight of my mum and dad standing on the touchline. They both looked pleased for me, but I could just *tell* that they still weren't speaking to each other. It was obvious from their body language. They were studiously not looking at each other and weren't even standing together. Lauren's dad, Mr Bell, was between them, with Lauren's dog, Chelsea, on her lead.

Suddenly my goals lost a bit of their gloss. Mum and Dad had had a stupid row over breakfast about, of all things, which one of them was going to drop me off at football, and who would take my twin sister Gemma to her ballet class. They seemed to argue all the time these days. Honestly, parents! Don't you just want to bang their heads together sometimes?

Although maybe I shouldn't be so quick to point the finger at my mum and dad, I thought ruefully. After all, Gemma and I had also had a *majorly* serious bust-up just last night. And it wasn't the first this week, either.

"GRACE!"

I jumped at the sound of Georgie's voice. I was so deep in thought, I hadn't realised that Melfield were about to kick off again.

"Wake up and smell the coffee, girl!" Georgie

yelled from right down the other end of the field. The parents standing around on the touchline grinned, and even Ria had a hint of a smile. "We've got to *concentrate*!"

"OK," I called back as Georgie, glaring sternly at me, pulled her baseball cap down more firmly over her amazing mass of black hair. I might be the Stars' captain, but Georgie's the bossy boots around here!

Anyway, I didn't want to think about my warring family just now, so I did as Georgie said and pushed the thoughts aside. At least I had my *best* mates around me, I consoled myself, as Melfield began passing the ball into our half. I liked all my other Springhill Stars team-mates, but Georgie, Katy, Hannah, Lauren, Jasmin and I were just the *closest*.

I'd joined the Stars when I was about nine, with my best friend Chloe, and that's when I first met Georgie. We got on OK, but we weren't particularly close friends because we didn't go to the same primary school. Jasmin and Lauren joined the Stars a while later, and I liked them both but again, I never got to know them that well because they didn't go to my school either. I didn't really have a special friend on the team for a little while because Chloe got bored with football and left to take up tennis.

But then everything just happened when Hannah and Katy joined the Stars earlier this year! Our coach at the time, the awesome Freya Reynolds, sent all six of us on an intensive football course for the first week of the Easter holidays and, oh my God, it was just so brilliant and the best thing *ever*. We got on so well and we had some huge laughs, but we also had some totally *massive* arguments. We're all so different, which is great, but it can sometimes lead to big trouble. I still have other school friends like Chloe, but I've *never* met a bunch of girls like Georgie and the others before. Sparks fly when we're together – and not always in a good way!

Melfield had been hassling our defence for the last five minutes, trying to pull a goal back. I'd moved a little way up the field, wondering if I needed to go and help defend, although I usually hung around in the centre circle. But Georgie had muscled her way between the Melfield strikers and was now clutching the ball firmly to her chest. I glanced across the field and could see that Jasmin was free on the left.

Sharp-eyed Georgie saw me glance Jasmin's way, and immediately she tossed the ball in her direction. That was one of the best things about being such good mates – it made our football heaps better!

Jasmin trapped the ball neatly and then set off up the field, a determined look on her face. Instantly I turned and ran up the pitch just ahead of her. Hannah, Lauren and Ruby (one of our other team-mates) were also pounding along behind me.

"Go, Jasmin!" Georgie yelled from her goalmouth.

Jasmin hesitated slightly, then side-footed the ball inside to Hannah, who swung it immediately over to Lauren. Hannah's touch was a bit too hard, though, and Lauren couldn't stop the ball. It hit the Melfield player who was marking her and bounced out of play.

"Sorry, Lauren," Hannah panted.

"Bad luck, Han," called Mr Fleetwood, Hannah's dad. He was standing in the crowd with Mrs Fleetwood and Hannah's grandpa. Mr Fleetwood used to yell at Hannah all the time and put her off, but he's a lot better now!

Ria stopped the ball with her foot and passed it straight to Hannah who went to take the throw-in.

"Good teamwork, girls," Ria said, nodding approvingly at me, Lauren, Jasmin and Ruby as we hovered close by, waiting for the throw. "Keep it together, now, for the last few minutes, and those points are ours." Her piercing dark eyes met mine. "I'm relying on you, captain!"

I nodded. I was still a tiny bit wary of Ria. She was quite different in her coaching approach to Freya, whom we'd all adored. And for the first few weeks she'd shouted a lot, too, just like Mr Fleetwood. But I was getting used to her now she'd reined herself in a bit, and so were the others. Apart from Georgie, who only just tolerated her. Mind you, Ria was dating Georgie's dad, Mr Taylor, which wasn't helping. And none of us had dared make any jokes about Ria maybe becoming Georgie's stepmother – Georgie would have ripped our heads off!

The Melfield defenders milled around us as Hannah took the throw, so she had no choice but to send it back down the field to Katy. I saw Katy spot a space ahead of us, a space that the Melfield defence weren't covering, and I began to run forward again.

I got away from the girl defending me, just as Katy sent a beautifully weighted ball towards me. As I ran into the empty space, it dropped almost at my feet and I latched onto it like it was superglued to my toes! There wasn't a single defender near me, except the goalie ahead, and she looked *very* nervous as I raced towards her penalty area.

Come on, Grace! Right or left? Decide! NOW!

Both of my goals so far had spun into the left-hand side of the net. What would the goalie be expecting me to do? These thoughts rushed through my head in the space of just a few seconds.

I saw the goalie move very slightly towards the left, so I let fly towards the right-hand corner. The ball shot into the goal, just nicking the post on the way.

"Hat-trick!" I heard Dad yell. "That's my girl! You're a star, Gracie!"

About two seconds later the ref blew his whistle. The rest of the team – Georgie, Hannah, Lauren, Katy, Jasmin, Jo-Jo, Emily, Debs, Ruby and Alicia – all zoomed towards me, shrieking with joy, and began slapping me on the back.

"Ow!" I said, although I was laughing, "That kind of *hurts*, guys!"

"Golden Girl Grace strikes again!" Jasmin announced. "Literally, ha ha!"

"Oh, *don't* call me that, Jasmin," I groaned. "It's totally embarrassing!"

The Melfield players were trudging off the field

past us, looking very disappointed. They were hoping for promotion too, but they were only fifth in our league at the moment.

"Sorry, Grace," Jasmin replied, her eyes dancing. "But I don't mean it *nastily*."

"Of course she doesn't," Hannah said cheerfully. "When I first met you, Grace, I nicknamed you the Perfect Princess!"

I pulled a face as we all turned to leave. "God, you make me sound like a real prize prat," I complained.

"Well, *look* at you, Grace," Jasmin went on, pointing a finger at me. "You're tall and you have gorgeous blonde hair and long legs and you look like a supermodel and you're fab at football—"

"*And* you're a really nice person, too." Georgie gave me what was meant to be a friendly punch on the shoulder – I think. "And believe me, I don't say *that* about many people."

I had to smile. I wondered what the girls would think if they'd seen me and Gemma yelling at each other last night. They wouldn't think I was a golden girl or a perfect princess *then*. We'd started fighting and Gemma had got a handful of my hair and wouldn't let go…

"That Grace Kennedy is *such* a pain in the bum," said a sneery voice behind us.

"I know," another voice agreed. "She *so* thinks she's all that."

My smile faded instantly as I half-glanced round and saw Rhiannon Marsh and Verity Blaine, two of the Melfield players, just behind us. Had they meant me to hear their bitchy comments? I wasn't sure, but it made me feel a bit sick and upset all the same. This kind of thing happened every so often, but I just tried to ignore it.

Georgie instantly whipped round to confront the other two girls. "Say that again to our faces, why don't you?" she demanded.

"It's OK, Georgie—" I began. But Hannah, Katy, Jasmin and Lauren had turned to stare at Rhiannon and Verity, as well.

"Now, *don't* make Georgie angry," Lauren told them solemnly. "You won't like her when she's angry, believe me."

"Oh, but it's understandable, isn't it, girls?" Jasmin said with a cheeky grin. "I mean, Grace *is* all that, isn't she?"

"Yes, Grace is gorgeous, so we can see why you might be jealous," Hannah said kindly.

Rhiannon and Verity scowled.

"We're *not* jealous—" Rhiannon muttered.

"Oh, you so are!" Lauren exclaimed.

"Never mind," Katy said, "Maybe one day you two will be brilliant footballers like Grace. If you practise every day. And night."

"But you'll never be as beautiful and as brainy and as talented as Grace, so you'll just have to suck it up and live with it," Georgie finished jauntily. "Good luck with that."

Rhiannon and Verity were both bright red by now. They'd never seen the Springhill Stars in action *off* the field before! I tried not to laugh as they pushed past us and rushed off to the changing-room.

"Thanks, guys," I said gratefully, "but you didn't have to do that."

"Yes, we totally *did*," Hannah broke in.

"Divided we stand, united we fall," Jasmin added, linking arms with me. She frowned. "Or is it the other way round?"

"Girls, I'm thrilled with your performance today!" Ria announced, coming to meet us as we reached the door. She was smiling from ear to ear. "It was a good home win, and it means three more points in the bag. Well done, all of you."

"Did the Blackbridge Belles win, too?" Katy asked. The Belles were our biggest local rivals and – wouldn't you just know it – they were top of our league at the moment. At the start of today, we'd been six points behind them, although we had a game in hand (one of our matches earlier in the season had been cancelled because the pitch was waterlogged).

Ria pulled a face and nodded. "I got a text. They beat the Swallows one-nil."

"Oh, b—" Georgie hastily swallowed down the swearword she'd been about to let fly. "*Blast*."

"Well *we* won, that's the main thing," Ria said briskly. "It means we're keeping the Belles in our sights. See you all at training on Tuesday." She glanced at Georgie. "But I might see *you* later this evening, if you're home."

"Fine," Georgie muttered, forcing a smile.

"Is Ria going out with your dad tonight?" Jasmin asked nosily as Ria strode off.

"Yep." This time it was Georgie's turn to pull a face. Jasmin opened her mouth to ask another question, and I elbowed her gently in the ribs. Looking a bit glum, Georgie sped up and disappeared down the corridor that led to the changing-room.

"I know, I know," Jasmin sighed, rolling her eyes. "I was about to put my foot in it yet again. Thanks, Grace."

"Any time, Jas," I laughed. Jasmin is lovely, but she can be a bit dippy and ditsy, and she doesn't always start up her brain before she puts her mouth in gear (her words, not mine!). I guess I'm kind of the peacemaker in the group, probably because I'm the oldest. I was thirteen at the end of September, and none of the others have their birthdays for a few months yet.

As I held the door open for the others, I took a quick look back across the pitch at Mum and Dad. They were standing next to each other now, but even from this distance I could tell that they were having another row about something or other, although they were doing it quietly so that no one around them noticed. But *I* could tell. What could they *possibly* have found to argue about at a Springhill Stars match? I wondered anxiously. But then, my parents argued about anything and everything these days, and it had been like that for months. They were obviously having big problems, but I didn't want to think about that, and where it might lead... I couldn't.

With a heartfelt sigh, I slipped through the doors and down the corridor to the changing-room.

We'd won and I'd scored a hat-trick, but somehow I couldn't totally enjoy it. I had a bad feeling about all this, like a black cloud was hanging over me, and suddenly the future seemed very uncertain.

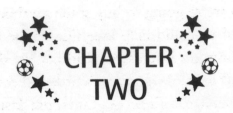

CHAPTER TWO

Usually I loved the buzz in the changing-room after a win – it kept me on a high all weekend. But today I felt a bit down, probably because of everything that was happening with Mum and Dad.

"We're still meeting up at the pool at the leisure centre tomorrow, right?" Hannah asked as the six of us made our way out of the changing-room and through the grounds of Melfield College to the car park. All of the Springhill Stars teams play their home games on the college pitches. "So what's everyone doing for the rest of today?"

"Mum's taking me shopping." Jasmine said

glumly, zipping up her bright pink fleecy jacket.

"Why so gloomy?" Lauren teased, tweaking Jasmin's bouncy pony-tail. "I thought you loved shopping."

"It's not *that* kind of shopping," Jasmin grumbled. "My parents think I need to do extra maths, so we're going to buy some textbooks."

None of us could help laughing at the disgusted look on Jasmin's face as she said her goodbyes and trudged off towards her mum's little red car. Mr and Mrs Sharma are both accountants, but Jasmin *hates* maths.

"Katy, do you want a lift home?" Jasmin called over her shoulder.

Katy shook her head. "I'm not going straight home," she replied, with the sweet smile that always transformed her serious face. "Have a lovely weekend, you guys." And she hurried out of the car park.

You might have noticed that Katy didn't say where she was going *or* what she was doing this weekend. Sometimes she can be a bit of a mystery girl. The only things we really know for sure about her is that her family are Polish, and they moved to England a few years ago. She has a mum, a dad and a little brother, but none of them ever come to the matches. Oh, and we know that she's a brilliant defender, too!

I looked towards the far end of the car park where Dad had parked. He was standing outside, leaning against the car, reading his newspaper. Mum was inside, talking on her mobile. I sighed. It didn't look like they'd made up yet.

"I'm going home to chill out in our hot tub in the garden," Lauren said. "Some of my cousins are coming over, and Dad's taking us all out to dinner."

"Oh, the lifestyle of the rich and famous!" Georgie said, raising her eyebrows. She's always teasing Lauren about how much money the Bells have got, but it's true – their lifestyle *is* a lot like a celebrity's! "I bet we'll be reading all about it in *OK!* magazine very soon."

"Shut it, you," Lauren said, poking her tongue out at Georgie. But luckily she wasn't offended because she and Georgie both have fearsome tempers and they've had some HUGE rows in the past few months. "And by the way, I've been meaning to ask you, are you practising putting your make-up on every day, like we showed you?"

Georgie groaned loudly. She's a real tomboy, but

somehow we'd talked her into letting us give her a makeover last month. Georgie had bought some new clothes and make-up, but mostly she still turned up at matches and for training nights in her tracksuit and Spurs shirt with only a slight hint of lip-gloss.

"Yikes! I'm later than late!" Georgie exclaimed, glancing at her watch and neatly avoiding Lauren's question. "Dad's taking me and my brothers to visit our gran. See you at the leisure centre tomorrow, guys." And she whizzed off, humming the theme tune to *Match of the Day*. Lauren, Hannah and I grinned as she jumped into the back of her dad's car. Her older brother Luke, who sometimes came to watch our games, was sitting in the front seat, and Georgie instantly leaned forward and flicked his baseball cap off his head. The two of them were fighting even before Mr Taylor pulled out of the car park.

"I thought Georgie said that she and Luke were getting on a lot better these days?" Hannah remarked, shaking her head.

"They are, but they'll always be arguing about something or other," Lauren replied. "Georgie'd never give in to a *boy*."

"You know what, I can't wait for Georgie to get interested in boys," I remarked a bit naughtily. "That's going to be a sight well worth seeing!"

"Georgie? Boys?" Lauren scoffed. "Are you mad, Grace? Can you *really* see Georgie fluttering her eyelashes at some poor unsuspecting guy?"

"She's more likely to give him a punch on the nose!" Hannah slung her sports bag over her shoulder. "See you tomorrow."

"What are you up to this afternoon?" I called after Hannah as she went over to her dad's car.

"Avoiding Olivia," Hannah replied gloomily. "She's studying for her mock GCSEs, and a bigger drama queen there never was."

Lauren and I giggled. Poor Hannah just doesn't get along with her stepsister, Olivia, who moved in with the Fleetwoods earlier this year.

"'Bye, Grace." Lauren peeled off in the opposite direction towards Mr Bell's big shiny silver Mercedes. "See you Tuesday."

So here was the moment I hadn't been looking forward to. I was now all on my own with my warring parents, and looking at the grim expressions on their faces sent my heart sinking like a stone. How much longer could they go on arguing like this? Why couldn't they just get along like they used to?

Dad glanced up from his newspaper and saw me. At least he brightened up a bit *then*.

"Here we are, the hat-trick heroine! Well done, love."

"Thanks, Dad."

It's because of Dad that I got into football, really. I was always a daddy's girl when I was little, toddling around the house after him all the time. I got into the habit of watching football on the TV with him, and after that it was only a short step to having a kick-around in our back garden, just the two of us. Gemma joined in sometimes, but she was never really that interested. My dad's into sport himself (he teaches PE, as well as French) and when he realised how much I enjoyed footie, he started coaching me properly. That was when I was about four years old, so sometimes it feels like I've been playing football *for ever*!

Mum switched off her mobile and smiled at me as I opened the car door.

"Well done, darling. I'm really proud of you."

I love my mum *loads*, but I guess I'm closer to my dad in lots of ways. Not just because we're both mad footie fanatics, but because we're alike in other things, as well. I don't usually have much time for other sports, but when we go on holiday, I love to try new things with Dad like tennis, snorkelling, water-skiing and surfing. Mum's into keep-fit too, but in a different way. She used to be a professional dancer, and now she teaches aerobics part-time at one of the local gyms. Gemma's also totally into dance – she goes to ballet, tap and jazz dance classes, and she and Mum love musicals. They're just as close as me and Dad because of that, so I guess it all evens out.

"Shall I drive?" Dad reached for the car keys which lay on the dashboard.

"No," Mum retorted irritably, grabbing the keys a second before Dad did. "I'm sitting in the driver's seat, so *I'll* drive."

I could feel the knot of apprehension in my tummy getting tighter as Dad scowled.

"You *know* I prefer to drive when we're all out together, Carly—"

"Too late," Mum snapped, holding onto the keys tightly.

"Or maybe *I* should drive," I broke in with a feeble attempt at humour. But I had to do *something.* I could tell from my parents' faces that if this argument didn't stop right now, it could blow up into something huge. Something that wasn't really about car keys and who was driving...

Dad was about to say something else when he caught my eye. I knew I looked worried, and that seemed to pull him up short. Without speaking, he climbed into the passenger side and put on his seat belt. Meanwhile, Mum revved up the engine and, looking a little triumphant, edged her way out of the car park.

No one spoke on the way to collect Gemma from her dance class. I stared out of the car window, trying to talk myself out of the feelings of anxiety and dread that were threatening to overwhelm me. I knew that Mum and Dad were having huge problems, but they *had* to sort them out. They just had to. I was clinging to the hope that maybe one day very soon, things would start to get better and we'd be a happy family again.

But if my parents didn't want to be together – didn't even seem to *like* each other – then what was going to happen?

The dance school was held in a huge old red-brick Victorian house that had been converted into studios upstairs and downstairs. As we pulled up at the kerb, we saw Gemma waiting for us outside the stained-glass front door. We're identical twins and people always do a double-take when they see us together because we look exactly alike – we're both tall and slim and we both have blue eyes and our long blonde hair is the same length. Mum used to dress us in matching outfits when we were little, but we try to make ourselves look as different as possible now. Gemma usually ties her hair up because I always wear mine loose, except when I'm playing footie.

We've been different characters for most of our lives, too. I was the confident, sociable twin (still am, I hope!), and Gemma was much more the quiet one. It took Mum *ages* to persuade Gemma to go to dance classes because, although she loved dancing around at home, she was *really* shy. She only started when she was nine, and for months she used to try and hide at the back of the class. But last year her dance school put on a production of *Grease*, and, to our surprise, Gemma was given the lead role of Sandy. She had to sing and dance and act and *everything*, and she was so nervous, none of us thought she'd be able to do it. She did, though – and she was brilliant! She'd even appeared in the local newspaper.

I sighed quietly as Gemma waved and ran towards the car. Ever since her success in the show, Gemma had begun to change. She was gradually becoming more and more confident and outgoing herself, and, although I was pleased for her, it was hard for me to get used to that. Suddenly, everything we did seemed to be a competition between us.

I think that's why we've started fighting more often...

"Hiya," Gemma called. She was smiling, but her smile faded instantly as she glanced swiftly at Mum and Dad before climbing into the back seat with me. She raised her eyebrows and I shook my head slightly. Like I told you, we'd had a *stupid* row yesterday – over a CD of Gem's that had gone missing, of all things – and we hadn't really made it up this morning, either. But now it was all forgotten. Now we were on the same side, wondering what was going to happen with Mum and Dad...

"How was football?" Gemma asked. I knew she was doing it just to break the tense silence.

"Good," I replied brightly. "We won 3-0."

"Don't be so modest, Gracie." Mum braked to a halt at a set of traffic lights. "It was *you* who scored all three goals."

"Ace, Grace!" Gemma said. It was an old family joke (OK, so it was never *that* funny), and I forced a smile. Now it was my turn.

"How was dance class?"

"Cool," Gemma replied. "I think I need new ballet shoes though, Mum."

"Fine," said Mum.

Silence again. God, this was worse than death by slow torture. I sneaked a sideways look at Gemma, and I could see that she was thinking exactly the same thing. Even though we haven't been getting on so well recently, we can still read each other's minds and moods pretty accurately.

"*Carla!*" Dad snapped suddenly, making us all jump. "Watch out for that cyclist!"

"I'm nowhere near him," Mum said in a clipped tone, glancing at the young man on the bike wobbling along on our left.

"You were too close," Dad retorted. "You don't have *any* idea how wide this car is, do you?"

"I didn't hit him, did I?" Mum yelled, losing her cool super-quickly. "For God's sake, it's no wonder I can't concentrate on driving with you going on at me all the time!"

"I am NOT going on at you!" Dad yelled back.

"All I'm saying is—"

"Whatever you're saying, I don't want to hear it," Mum broke in. She was fuming, I could hear it in her voice. "Just *leave* it, Will."

I didn't look at Gemma, but I could almost *feel* her anxiety and tension alongside my own. We drew up outside the house and got out of the car in silence.

"Did anyone feed Lewis before we left?" Dad asked as he unlocked the door. We could hear Lewis in the hall, barking his head off.

"Mum said she would," Gemma replied.

Mum looked instantly guilty. "I forgot," she muttered.

"Oh, for God's sake!" Dad looked disgusted as Lewis rushed to greet us. "No wonder the poor mutt's making such a racket."

"Look, I had lots to do this morning before we left," Mum said coldly.

I knelt down and patted Lewis's white and black spotted coat. I didn't think I could stand this for a *minute* longer.

"That's why I told you not to come with us to the game." Dad looked self-righteous. "Me and Gracie could have gone on our own, like we usually do."

"Oh, so what am I, some sort of house slave?" Mum snapped, her face turning red. "I have to do *everything* around here—"

"Stop it!" Gemma yelled. "Stop it, stop it, STOP IT!"

There was an electric silence. I stood up, shoulder to shoulder with Gemma, glad that she'd said something, but worried about what would happen next. I was the older twin by seven minutes and, like I said, I'd always been more outgoing and confident than Gemma. But it was Gem who'd spoken up.

"Gemma—" Mum began.

"Why aren't you getting along any more?" Gemma broke in urgently. "What's going on? Are you going to split up? Tell us! Me and Grace have a right to know!"

I froze. Immediately I switched my gaze from Gemma's white, tense face to Mum and Dad. The possibility of our parents splitting up was something I hadn't allowed myself to think about too much because it simply *wasn't* going to happen. That was what I'd told myself, over and over again. I waited for Mum and Dad to reply – for the denials, the reassurances, the explanations that they were just 'going through a bad patch'...

None of those things came. Mum and Dad both looked hugely guilty, sheepish and apprehensive. They glanced at each other as if neither of them knew what to say. I'd never seen them look so serious before. I was ice-cold all over and shaking.

"What's happening?" I asked in a trembling voice.

"You tell them what we've decided, Will," Mum murmured, unable to look us in the eye.

"Tell us *what*?" Gemma demanded.

Dad looked supremely uncomfortable.

"Well, your mum and I—" He stopped and cleared his throat. "We weren't going to tell you just yet until we'd sorted out all the details. But, yes, girls, your mum and I have decided that it's better for all of us if we have a trial separation..."

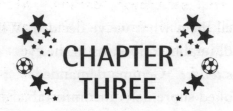

CHAPTER THREE

Separation...

As I lay on my bed, that word kept running through my head over and over again. Just one little word, but it meant that everything had been broken up and blown apart. It spelt the end of our family life as I knew it...

Tears started to fill my eyes and I gulped and swallowed and bit them back. I'd already cried far too much, and my eyes were red and sore. But I just couldn't stop re-living the moment when Mum and Dad had told us the horrible news.

"You're splitting up!" Gemma had exclaimed,

looking totally devastated. Then she'd started crying noisily, just like a little kid.

I'd stared at Mum and Dad, numb with shock. I didn't even realise that tears were rolling down my face until a few minutes later, when one dropped off the end of my nose and splashed onto my hand.

"It's a trial separation, darling," Mum said in a voice shaking with emotion. "Your dad and I want to work things out, but at the moment that isn't looking very likely. So we think some time apart, maybe a couple of months or longer, might help us to decide what we really want to do."

"Look, girls, I know this isn't something you wanted to hear," Dad added, looking wretched. "And it's something we *all* have to get used to, but—"

"We still love you to bits, both of you," Mum broke in. Her face was pale and distressed, and she was crying too. "This has *nothing* to do with you girls, believe me—"

"But can't you try again without separating?" I blurted out. "Try to make things better?" I racked my brains for a solution. "You could go to counselling—?"

"We're arranging that, too," Mum assured me.

"But – well – your dad and I still feel that a trial separation is for the best at the moment."

Gemma was sobbing even harder. Her face was all screwed up, reminding me of when she was very small and she'd fallen over in the park and hurt her knee. Mum went over to put her arms around her, but Gemma pushed her away and fled upstairs.

"You girls need time to get your heads around all this," Dad mumbled, looking as guilty as if he'd just murdered someone. "We'll talk again when you've got over the shock, OK, Gracie?"

I nodded. I didn't feel able to speak. I followed Gemma upstairs and went into my own bedroom and shut the door. I'd been lying here for an hour or two now, crying every so often and listening to Gemma sobbing in the room next door.

The D-word – divorce – hadn't been mentioned by anyone yet, but it was what we were all thinking about...

I laced my hands behind my head and thought about my friends whose parents had split up and then divorced. There were quite a few. Chloe's mum and dad had separated when she was a baby. A couple of my friends in my class at Greenwood Comprehensive also had parents who'd divorced.

And they all seemed OK with it. Chloe had told me once that she loved visiting her dad because he always took her out to fab places and bought her fantastic presents.

But divorce was something that happened to other people. I didn't want it to happen to MY family. A trial separation was bad enough.

Come on, Grace, think positive! I told myself. At least my mum and dad were fit and healthy. Georgie's mum had died a few years ago, and even though Georgie seemed OK, I think she was still getting over it.

Typical me. I always try to see both sides of an argument and end up driving myself CRAZY. Why didn't I just admit it? I wanted to have a flaming tantrum and scream and shout and yell at my parents NOT to give up on our family!

So much for Grace the Golden Girl, the Perfect Princess…

There was a tiny tap at my door.

"Who is it?" I called. I didn't feel ready to speak to Mum and Dad just yet.

"Me." Gemma didn't wait for an invitation to come in, she simply slipped inside. Lewis was at her heels. She sat down on the end of my bed and

I could see her eyes were red-rimmed and swollen. Lewis, meanwhile, slumped down on the bedside rug with a sigh, as if he too knew what was going on.

"You OK?" I asked, just for something to say, because I knew she *wasn't*.

Gemma didn't even bother to answer.

"What do you think's going to happen next?" she asked.

I shrugged. "No idea."

Gemma stared hard at me. "Had Dad said anything to you about all this before today?"

"No!" I said, shocked that she'd even think that. "I found out about it just now, same as you."

There was silence. Then another knock at the door made us both jump almost out of our skins. Mum looked in.

"Er – girls, there are a few other things we need to discuss," she said in a quiet voice, with a hint of pleading. "Can we come in?"

I glanced uncertainly at Gemma.

"Oh, why not?" Gemma muttered sulkily. "I think we've been kept in the dark for long enough, don't you, Grace?"

I nodded.

Mum came in, with Dad behind her. I guessed they'd been talking about the situation downstairs, wondering how best to approach us. And as far as I knew, not having heard any shouting, they hadn't been rowing about it, either. So if they could talk without arguing about *that*, then why couldn't they just get along together more often?

"Why didn't you tell us what was going on?" I burst out. "If Gem hadn't asked, when *were* you going to tell us?"

Mum and Dad looked upset and embarrassed.

"We'd decided to wait for a few weeks until half-term," Dad explained haltingly. "We thought there'd be more time then to discuss everything and talk things through. It's been a bit of a strain, though, to be honest, girls."

"We know that there's still a lot of talking to do," Mum added nervously. "But there are a few practicalities we have to discuss."

"Like what?" I asked, a feeling of doom chilling my bones.

"Well, obviously one of us has to move out of the house." Dad couldn't look me or Gemma in the eye. "Your mum and I have decided that it's best if I go."

I'd already realised, with dread, that this was

bound to happen. After all, people couldn't have a trial separation and still live in the same house together. But hearing Dad say it aloud was still a huge shock.

"When are you going?" I asked miserably.

"Not for a few weeks yet, Gracie." Dad rushed to reassure me. "Your mum and I have agreed that I'll stay until half-term, which is what we originally planned. But even after that I'll still be close by. I'm going to be temporarily moving in with Bryan from school, then I'll find a place to rent. But I'll still come round here and see you and Gemma every day—"

"And we're supposed to be *grateful*?" I said shakily.

Gemma was staring at Dad with big wide eyes, as if she couldn't quite believe what she was hearing. "Don't go, Dad!" Gemma pleaded. She didn't look as if she had any more tears left in her, but they were beginning to run down her cheeks again. I began to sob, too. My whole world was collapsing in ruins around me.

Mum and Dad were crying now. They came over to the bed, and this time they hugged us both, one after the other, without anyone pushing anyone away. Even Lewis joined in, putting his front paws on the bed and rubbing his cold nose against my leg.

"Have you told the rest of the family, yet?" I asked, scrubbing at my wet face with a crumpled tissue. "What about Gran and Gramps and Nan and Grandpa?"

Mum and Dad both shook their heads.

"Why not?" Gemma demanded, a bit aggressively.

"As we've decided that your dad will stay until half-term, we don't really need to tell anyone yet," Mum explained. "It also gives you two more time to get used to the idea a little more."

"There are a lot of people who are going to need to know," Dad said. "Not just family, but friends and work colleagues and so on. We wanted to sort out the practical details first before we tell everybody."

I guessed that Mum and Dad were worried about the rest of the family trying to interfere. Mum's parents, Gran and Gramps, are lovely, but they *do* like to stick their noses in sometimes and tell everyone what they *should* be doing.

Gemma was pouting mutinously.

"So you don't want *us* to tell anyone then," she muttered.

"Girls, we'd never ask you to do that," Mum replied gently. "We simply think it might be easier if we have some space and time to discuss things, just the four of us."

I nodded, even though my first instinct had been to grab my phone straightaway and pour my heart out to Katy, Hannah, Lauren, Jasmin and Georgie, as well as some of my other friends. But now I was having second thoughts. Mum was right. I needed time alone to think about this horrible situation and try to make some sense of it, any way I could.

Golden Girl Grace, the Perfect Princess. Not so golden and perfect now, though... Lauren, Katy and the others would feel sorry for me, and I couldn't bear that. No, I didn't want to tell them yet. I didn't want to tell *anyone*.

Besides, it was still a few weeks to half-term. Mum and Dad might change their minds before then and decide to stay together, I thought with desperate hope. Then everything would be all right again. Maybe the same thing had occurred to Gem, because now she was nodding, too.

"OK," she agreed. "I won't tell anyone. Not for the moment, anyway."

"Now, your dad's going to make lunch." Mum

moved a strand of hair tenderly off my face. "We'll talk some more later, after we've eaten."

"OK then, girls, lunch in twenty minutes," Dad said, and he and Mum left in silence.

"I think I'll heave if I eat anything," Gemma said morosely, stroking Lewis's ears.

"Me, too." I couldn't understand how, in the space of just a couple of hours, my whole life as I knew it had been torn apart. It was a gut-wrenching feeling.

Gemma's eyes narrowed. "I wonder if Dad's having an affair?" she blurted out.

"*Gemma!*" I could hardly believe my ears. "What are you talking about? Of *course* he isn't!"

"How do *you* know?" Gemma retorted. "He's the one who's moving out, isn't he?"

I gave her a shove and she tumbled off my bed. I was so mad, I couldn't help it.

"Dad wouldn't do something like that!" I shouted at her. "I don't know how you can even *think* such a thing—"

Her face absolutely furious, Gemma jumped to her feet.

"I can think what I like, Grace Kennedy!" she shot back. "We might be twins, but we don't have to be *exactly* the same all the time. We don't *have* to look the same or think the same or act the same. In fact, to be honest, I'm sick and tired of being your twin sister!"

And she stalked out of the room. Shaking, I curled up on my bed as Lewis jumped to his feet, looking unhappy, unable to decide whether to follow Gemma or stay with me.

What was happening to my family?

"Water slide – right now!" Georgie ordered, grabbing Jasmin's hand and beginning to tow her across the pool.

"No, Georgie!" Jasmin squealed in mock-terror, "Not the *big* one!"

Lauren, Katy, Hannah and I burst into giggles as Georgie continued to tow Jasmin through the water towards the tallest of the three slides. It was Sunday lunchtime, and Mr and Mrs Fleetwood, Hannah's parents, had brought us to the leisure centre and then gone off to sit in the café. The leisure centre was brand-new and we *loved* going there. The pool was enormous and it was inside a big dome with a glass roof, so that you could float on your back and look up at the sky. We'd slid down the slides, we'd been drenched by the water cannon and we'd battled with the wave machine. Now the four of us were sitting in the huge, bubbly, blue and white tiled spa pool, watching while Georgie bullied Jasmin up the steps of the absolutely *massive* slide. She'd chickened out of trying it earlier because of the long queues. The pool had been mega-busy when we first arrived, but now a lot of the swimmers had gone off to have lunch.

"Go, Jasmin!" Hannah yelled.

Jasmin was pretending to be incredibly nervous – or maybe she *wasn't* pretending! She sat down at the top and Georgie gave her a push. Closing her eyes and holding her nose, Jasmin flew down the slide with a loud, terrified shriek that echoed around the dome and made us all collapse into hysterical laughter. Georgie was close behind her. They zoomed into the water and landed in a tangle of arms and legs with a massive *splash*.

"Oh, that was *scary*!" Jasmin panted, as she and Georgie swam over to us. "But it was so *fun*!"

I smiled. I have a big soft spot for Jas because she's always so sweet and upbeat and just – well – *happy*. That was exactly what I needed right now. I'd thought about not coming today, but I was glad

I hadn't cancelled. Being with the other girls was making me feel a little better, even though I hadn't said a word about what happened yesterday with Mum and Dad. It was on my mind all the time, though. How could it not be? Yesterday Dad had moved all his stuff out of his and Mum's bedroom, and now he was sleeping in the spare room until he moved out.

"Anyone want to have a race?" Georgie asked eagerly, flicking a foamy bubble at Katy.

"I might," Katy replied, "if you're not going to cheat again, Miss Taylor."

"Ooh, that is *so* unfair!" Georgie exclaimed, trying to look innocent, and failing miserably. "It was all Lauren's fault – she didn't get the starting bit right."

"You are *such* a liar, liar, pants on fire, Georgie." Lauren rolled her eyes. "You'd set off before I'd even *started* to say, 'Ready, steady, go'."

"That's because the water gets in my ears and makes me a bit deaf," Georgie explained.

"Oh, you're so full of it, Georgie," Lauren scoffed.

"Sorry, I didn't quite catch that?" Georgie shot back, and we all grinned.

I'll tell you something, if you didn't know us at all and you saw us at the leisure centre pool right now, you'd be able to guess lots about us, just from looking at our swimwear!

Georgie was wearing an old black shapeless swimsuit that looks like it might have belonged to her granny, and her wild hair was screwed up on top of her head with an ancient scrunchie.

Lauren's bikini was turquoise and silver (designer, of course). She'd brought a matching sarong and flip-flops which she'd left at the poolside, and her blonde hair had been neatly secured on top of her head with some kind of amazing accessory that looked like a pair of chopsticks.

Jasmin's one-piece was *so* Jasmin! It was lilac with pink spots and it had these cute little ruffles on the shoulders and a little retro frilly skirt. She even had a matching headband and flip-flops. There wasn't another outfit like it in the whole pool.

Meanwhile, Hannah's and Katy's bikinis were stylish and pretty, but sensible – just like they were. Although I guessed that Hannah's had probably cost a lot more than Katy's. Katy's family don't seem to have much money to spare, and sometimes she doesn't always come along to the pool with us because it's quite expensive to get in. But I was glad she'd come today.

As for me, I hadn't felt like putting as much effort into my appearance as I usually did. But I'd washed my hair and blow-dried it to a sleek, shiny finish the day before, so it still looked quite good. And I was wearing my favourite bikini, which was a metallic gold colour. I thought I looked OK. And, I suddenly realised, someone else obviously did too...

A boy was sitting on the edge of the main pool, kicking his legs in the water, and he was staring at me very intently. I pretended not to notice, but I could just see him out of the corner of my eye. I saw him turn his head to glance down to the other end of the pool, and that was when I sneaked a quick look at him. My heart skipped a beat. He was *gorgeous*!

Dark, silky hair down to his shoulders, all long and ruffled and wet, taller than me but not too skinny with it. A bit tanned. About a year or so older than me. Wearing black swim shorts.

"Our game in hand against the Kingswood Cats at the beginning of half-term is going to be mega-important," Georgie was saying. "Because if we can beat *them*, and then thrash the Belles the following

Saturday, we'll be joint top of the league!"

"Yeah, but remember some of us won't be here for the Cats game," Lauren pointed out. "My mum and dad are taking me to France on holiday the day school breaks up."

"And we're going to Scotland to see my grandparents, so I'll miss it, too," Hannah added apologetically. "But only for a few days. I'll be back for the Belles game."

"So will I," Lauren agreed.

Georgie groaned loudly. We didn't usually have games on both Saturdays of the half-term week because often a lot of the players were away with their families. But this time we had the rescheduled game against the Kingswood Cats to play, as well as the crucial game against the Blackbridge Belles.

"Do you *have* to go on holiday?" Georgie complained, only half-jokingly.

I wasn't really listening as Lauren said something in reply and the others laughed. I was still staring at the boy when suddenly he turned back and caught my eye. I immediately looked away, feeling myself colour up to the roots of my hair.

"Don't you think so, Grace?"

I started as Hannah said my name.

"Er – sorry?" I mumbled. "I didn't quite get that."

Georgie stared at me, perplexed.

"What planet are you on, Grace?" she demanded, raising her eyebrows. "I said we should discuss our tactics for the match against the Belles – and you're not even listening!"

"Why are you so red, Grace?" Jasmin asked curiously. "You're blushing."

"No, I'm not, I'm really not," I replied quickly, feeling myself flush even pinker. But I *had* to know if the gorgeous guy was still staring at me, and without making it too obvious, I flicked a quick look in his direction. He was!

Lauren, who was next to me in the spa pool, began to giggle.

"That boy fancies Grace!" she declared loudly. "He's staring at her!"

"Which boy?" Jasmin turned round eagerly to have a good look.

"Don't be an idiot, Lauren!" I mumbled, as the others shrieked with laughter. I could have *died* when they ALL turned round to stare. It was all I could do not to sink right down into the bubbles out of sight!

I cast an anxious glance at the boy. Looking a bit embarrassed himself, he stood up and dived neatly into the water with hardly a splash. Then he swam away up the pool towards the slides. He was a fantastic swimmer – strong, fast and powerful.

"Oh, sorry, Grace. Looks like we've scared him off!" Georgie spluttered through gales of raucous laughter.

"God, you lot are so—" I stopped myself just in time. I was going to say 'childish', but I settled on "You're so *daft* sometimes."

"Do you want to *kiss* him, Grace?" Jasmin asked solemnly. But there was a mischievous twinkle in her eyes. "I wonder what it's like. To kiss a boy, I mean."

Georgie made a fearsome noise as if she was going to be sick, and we all laughed. But secretly, I really *did* think they were being a bit childish. Although we sometimes discussed pop stars and soap stars and other celebs we thought were cute, none of the other girls had ever had a boyfriend. They just seemed to treat going out with a boy as a big joke! Some of the girls in my Year 8 class at school had boyfriends, though, and *they* didn't think there was anything odd about it. And because I was older than the others, I guess I was getting interested in boys a bit earlier than they were.

For the first time since I'd become best mates with the others, I silently wished that I'd been on my own. Maybe then the boy would have come over and chatted me up, I thought longingly. He wasn't likely to talk to me with five hysterically giggling girls watching his every move! Oh well, I probably wouldn't see him again, whoever he was. We didn't come to the leisure centre *that* often, because it was right over the other side of town, as well as being expensive. So that was that. Shame...

Although maybe it wasn't all bad, I suddenly realised. That boy had taken my mind off the situation at home for a little while. And that could only be a good thing.

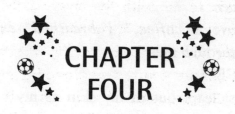

CHAPTER FOUR

"Oh, hi there!"

I was wandering through the shopping centre alone, just minding my own business, when I heard someone speaking to me.

I turned. There, looking even more gorgeous in jeans and a black hoodie, was the boy from the leisure centre pool. I was so shocked, I just stared at him in disbelief for a moment.

"I saw you on Sunday," the boy went on. "You were at the pool with your mates."

"Oh, yes, I was," I replied coolly, even though I was secretly thrilled to see him again. I was really

glad I'd blow-dried my hair and put my make-up on before I came out. I was wearing a denim miniskirt with a white wrap-around top and flat red shoes and lots of silver bangles. I knew I looked good!

"I was wondering if you fancied going for a coffee?" The boy smiled at me and my insides flipped over.

"I'd love a coffee," I breathed, excitement flooding through me.

"GRACE!"

I almost leapt out of my skin as my wonderful daydream was ever so rudely interrupted. I blinked. For a second I didn't know where I was, and then I remembered. Oh, yes – Tuesday night footie training!

Ria Jones was standing in front of me, throwing a ball from hand to hand. She looked highly annoyed. Meanwhile, the rest of the team were standing around with grins on their faces.

"Keep up, please, Grace!" Ria said in an irritated voice. "I just asked you to work with Lauren. I want 110 per cent concentration from *all* of you tonight."

"Sorry, Ria," I apologised.

Ria nodded curtly and then began to divide the

others up into pairs, handing a football to each couple as she did so.

"What are we supposed to be doing?" I asked Lauren in a low voice.

"God, Grace, what's the matter with you?" Lauren looked at me a bit anxiously. "Are you worrying about the match against the Blackbridge Belles?"

I almost laughed. Lauren just had *no* idea. Football was the last thing on my mind at the moment. I was totally *dreading* my dad moving out, and I'd kind of pushed it to the back of my mind, hoping that awful day would never come. After all, anything could happen in the next few weeks, so I didn't want to say anything to the others just yet. Telling people outside the family would make it all seem too real and final. But I was a bit worried that I'd just burst into tears and blurt the whole thing out if any of the other girls questioned me too closely.

So, to be honest, daydreaming about the boy at the swimming-pool was the only escape I had from all this stress at the moment.

The situation at home was doing my head in. Mum and Dad were being really polite to each other now, but Gemma and I were still at each other's throats. Gem was adamant that there must be more to the separation than we'd been told, and she kept going on about Dad maybe having a girlfriend. That *really* wound me up, and we'd had another fight about it last night.

I used to be able to lose myself in footie, but at the moment that was stressful, too, what with the game in hand and the Belles match coming up. I sighed quietly as I realised that the others would expect me to be on top form *and* bag a few goals into the bargain.

"I suppose I *am* worrying about the match, a bit," I replied, knowing that this was the safest answer.

"Don't worry, Grace, you'll be fantastic, as usual." Lauren slapped me cheerfully on the back. "We're relying on you to score the winning goal!"

See what I mean? More pressure.

"OK, get ready, please, girls," Ria called as Lauren and half of the other girls went over to the touchline. "You've done throw and return before, so you know how it works. Throw to your partner's chest, head and feet in turn, and vary the number of times the ball bounces – three, two and one. And remember the throw-in rules. Both feet must be on the ground when the ball is thrown, the hands must go directly over the head and the ball has to be thrown straight, no leaning to right or left. Off you go."

The other half of the couples formed a line standing opposite their partners, and I waited for the first throw from Lauren. It bounced three times before I caught it on my chest.

"I reckon we should spend the next few weeks discussing how we're going to totally *annihilate* the Blackbridge Belles," Georgie remarked as she neatly trapped a throw from Hannah. "We need a plan, guys."

"Georgie, we're playing the Shawcross Swallows *and* the Kingswood Cats before that," Katy pointed out sensibly, tossing the ball to Jasmin. "We can't just focus on one game."

"And the match right *after* the Belles is the second round of the County Cup," Hannah added. "We want to do well in that, too, don't we?"

Georgie looked thoughtful as she brought down another throw-in with her foot. "Yeah, but I think I'd rather get promotion than win the Cup."

"Me, too," Lauren agreed.

"Ooh, maybe we can do the double!" Jasmin suggested, her eyes shining.

I realised that Georgie was looking at me expectantly.

"Er – I think promotion would be fab," I said quickly, trying to sound as upbeat as possible. "A long run in the Cup would be good too, though."

Georgie rolled her eyes. "Sit on the fence, why don't you, Grace!"

"Well, that's what I think!" I said a bit snappily, and then instantly regretted it as I saw the girls glance at each other in surprise. "Sorry," I muttered, "I'm a bit tired."

"Oh, poor Grace," Jasmin said, looking concerned. "Is everything OK?"

"Sure," I said with a little laugh that sounded utterly fake, even to me. "Everything's fine."

"Has anyone else also looked at the fixtures list and noticed that our second game against the Blackbridge Belles is the *very* last game of the season?" Georgie pointed out. "That means if we can keep up with the Belles in the league, that last match could be the decider in who gets automatic promotion."

"Scary!" Jasmin remarked with a shudder. I didn't say anything. I could hardly think about what was going to happen next week, let alone next April, which was months away.

"Change places with your partners now, please," Ria called.

A bit later on, Ria taught us a dribbling drill we'd never tried before. She gave us each a ball and then marked out an area with cones that the whole team could fit into, with a bit of room to spare. Then she gave us coloured bands and told us to tuck them into the back of our shorts with just a few inches hanging out. The aim of the game was to dribble your ball around the marked out area and try to pull out other people's bands while keeping control of your own ball. If your band got pulled out, you had to leave the area.

I wasn't in the mood for footie training, but I had to admit this was pretty fun. It was quite difficult to watch where you were dribbling your own ball, and also look out for people trying to nick your band from you!

"This is to teach you to be aware of what's happening around you, even when you have the ball," Ria called. "Don't let your ball go out of the coned-off area either, or you're out!"

"I've got it!" Jasmin squealed triumphantly, holding up the band she'd just whipped from Ruby's shorts. "You're out, Ruby!"

"So are you!" giggled Katy. She'd just sneaked up behind Jasmin and stolen *her* band while Jas was distracted.

For the first time that night I actually began enjoying myself. I managed to keep my band until there was just me and Katy left. Ria had made the dribbling-area smaller and smaller by moving the cones inwards as more people were out, so it was getting quite tight.

Katy made a grab for my band, but I swerved around her. She came after me again but stumbled, and I managed to reach out and grab her band.

"Got it!" I laughed, holding it up in the air.

Katy grinned and slapped me on the back as the others cheered. "Well done, captain!"

I stared at her a *little* suspiciously. "You didn't lose on purpose, did you, just to try and cheer me up?"

Katy's eyes opened wide. "Why would I do that?" she enquired innocently. "You *said* everything was fine, didn't you?"

I managed a smile. The others had obviously guessed that there was something wrong, but they weren't pushing me to tell them what it was, and I was really grateful. I'd tell them when I felt ready. Or maybe I wouldn't have to explain at all, if only

Mum and Dad could work things out...

"About the Belles game," Georgie began as we made our way to the changing-room at the end of the session.

"Been thinking about the master plan, have you, Georgie?" Lauren asked with a grin.

"Well, I want to be prepared," Georgie retorted. "*I* was the one who got flattened by Lucy Grimshaw last time we played them, and I don't want that to happen again!"

Lauren looked a bit embarrassed. Lucy Grimshaw is the Belles' striker, and she's the original Tank Girl. She looks like she could stop a car with one hand, like a superhero. Anyway, when we played them last season, Lauren had been having a lot of problems at home that she hadn't told us about. She lost her temper during the game with Lucy Grimshaw and pushed her over into Georgie, who ended up getting injured.

I bit my lip as it occurred to me that *I* was having problems too, and I didn't want to tell the other girls about them, like Lauren hadn't. I hoped that wouldn't make me lose concentration and play badly, but I knew without a doubt that my mind just wasn't on football at the moment. It suddenly seemed so unimportant compared to everything else. My shoulders sagged slightly as we went into the changing-room. I wasn't sure I could cope with all this stress.

I wondered if the boy from the swimming-pool would mind if his girlfriend played football? I knew some guys thought women's football was all just a big joke. Georgie's brothers Luke and Jack used to tease her about playing footie all the time. But the swimming-pool boy looked a lot more sensitive than that.

"I saw Jacintha Edwards in the supermarket yesterday when I went shopping with Mum after school," Hannah remarked as we all stripped off our kit. Jacintha Edwards was the Blackbridge Belles' captain.

"Yeah?" Georgie was onto it like a shot. "Why didn't you say so before?"

"I forgot," Hannah replied a bit defensively.

"Did Jacintha say anything?" Georgie interrogated her. "Did she ask about our tactics for the match, or try to psych you out by playing mind games?"

"Not really." Hannah raised her eyebrows. "She and her mum were buying baked beans. Jacintha said Hi, and I said Hi back to her."

"Ooh, that sounds suspicious," Lauren remarked, grinning cheekily at Georgie.

"Shut it, smart-mouth!" Georgie retorted, whipping Lauren across the backside with the shirt that she'd just taken off. The others laughed, including me, although half my mind was on *the boy* as I tried to recall exactly what he looked like...

"How many tins of baked beans were Jacintha and her mum buying?" Jasmin asked curiously.

Hannah looked blank. "God, that is such a *Jasmin* question!" she exclaimed. "I don't know. Three or four?"

"Why on *earth* do you want to know that, Jasmin?" asked Katy.

"Oh, I just thought maybe Jacintha was hoping for some wind assistance so she can run faster!" Jasmin explained, a wicked twinkle in her eyes.

The others giggled, and I did too, but I was still thinking about HIM. *Was his hair just above his shoulders, or so long it touched them?*

"Are you staying here all night, Grace?" Lauren asked, poking me in the ribs.

I started. I looked around and realised that everyone else was almost dressed. In fact, Ruby,

Emily and Alicia were already leaving, yelling their goodbyes, and there I was standing in my pink bra and knickers.

"Sorry," I muttered, grabbing my black canvas skinnies and striped blue and white T-shirt. I was getting a lift home with Lauren because Mum had a late aerobics class to teach at the gym, and Dad had a staff meeting after school. I was quite relieved, to tell you the truth. It was impossible to have a normal conversation with either of them at the moment.

I got dressed in record time, not bothering with any make-up. It'd be just my luck to meet the gorgeous boy again on my way home when I wasn't looking my best, I reflected, as we piled out of the changing-room. I knew I was being ridiculous, though. I was going from the changing-room to the car park and being dropped off at our house! I wasn't likely to see him again anyway, unless we went back to the leisure centre, and even then there was only a small chance that he'd be there.

I felt quite depressed as we all said goodbye and Georgie reminded us to think up ideas for our Blackbridge Belles master plan.

"Grace, you've got that look on your face again," Lauren said as we walked to her dad's car.

"What look?"

"This one." Lauren put her head on one side and made her eyes go all dreamy and dopey. Despite my embarrassment, I couldn't help laughing.

"I do NOT look like that, Lauren Bell!"

"Oh yes you do," Lauren assured me. "You're not on the planet at the moment, are you, Grace?"

"I'm all right," I replied. "I'm just not getting on very well with Gemma, that's all."

That seemed the safest thing to say. And it *was* true.

"Why not?" Lauren slowed down a little so that we had a bit more time to chat before we reached the car. "I thought twins were always really close?"

"Well, we used to be..." Memories rushed through my mind, tumbling over each other. Gemma and I always sharing our sweets; talking in the special language we made up when we were seven; building a sandcastle together on the beach; standing up for each other against bullies in the playground; telling the hairdresser we both wanted our hair cut to the *exact* same length, and then checking it with the tape measure... Where had those two happy little girls gone?

"So what's different now?" Lauren wanted to know.

I sighed. "Gemma and I have changed, I suppose. Well, I haven't, but I think Gem has." I remembered my sister's words. *We might be twins, but we don't have to be exactly the same all the time.* "She's trying to be different from me."

"I thought you *were* different," Lauren pointed out. "I know you look the same, but she's all arty and creative, isn't she, while you're into sports and stuff?"

I nodded. "What I mean is, I don't think she wants to be a twin any more."

"It must be tough for her sometimes," Lauren said as we reached the car. "Gemma used to be a lot shyer and quieter than you, didn't she, Grace, until quite recently? Maybe she just wants to step out of your shadow."

"Maybe." I managed a rueful smile. "But it's almost like Gemma *blames* me for being the oldest twin, and for looking like her! I know it sounds daft, but that's how she makes me feel."

"Well, don't forget you're a hard act to follow, Grace!" Lauren said with a smile.

I thought about Lauren's remarks as I climbed into Mr Bell's car and buckled my seatbelt. I realised that Gemma wanted to separate from me a little more and become her own person, and that she was enjoying her new-found confidence. I could understand her need to work out her own identity as we grew up. That didn't mean I had to like it – I just had to learn to cope with it.

But now the Mum and Dad situation had been thrown into the mix, and it was already affecting my relationship with Gemma. Instead of becoming closer and supporting each other through it, we were drifting apart. And I had a feeling we hadn't seen the worst of it yet. Just call me Madame Grace who sees everything that's going to happen in the future in her crystal ball...

When the Bells dropped me off, I could see that Mum and Dad weren't home yet because their cars weren't in the drive. I opened the front door with my key, and a second later, Gemma charged out of the kitchen. Lewis was following right behind her, but at a more leisurely pace.

"What's going on?" I asked. Gemma's face was pale and looked as if she'd been crying.

"I'll tell you *exactly* what's going on," Gemma said in a trembling voice. "I know why Mum and Dad are separating. I was right – Dad has a *girlfriend*!"

CHAPTER FIVE

"You're a liar!" I burst out, "I don't believe you!"

Gemma stared at me aggressively. "It's true!" she snapped.

I clenched my fists. I was so furious and full of hurt, I wanted to slap Gemma's face, hard. The force of my feelings was scaring me.

"You've made it up—"

"No, I haven't!" Gemma shouted. She whipped something out of her pocket, and I saw that it was Dad's mobile phone. "Dad left this behind this morning, and I checked it out." She began pressing buttons. "He has loads of messages from someone called Lilly. Take a look."

My eyes opened wide. "You've *read* Dad's text messages?"

"Well, *duh*!" Gemma said nastily, "Of course I have! Mum and Dad aren't telling us much, are they? I want to know what's going on!"

"So do I, but I wouldn't go snooping and sneaking around—"

"Oh, but that's you all over, isn't it?" Gemma jeered. "Goodie-goodie Grace who doesn't *ever* put a foot wrong. Miss Prim and Proper, butter-wouldn't-melt-in-her-mouth—"

"Shut up, Gemma!" I yelled. We were going way off track here. This wasn't about me and Gemma, whatever Gemma thought, this was about Mum and Dad.

I snatched the phone from her and stared at the screen. *Hi Will, fancy a drink 2morrow nite? Lilly x*

"And that's just one of them," Gemma said triumphantly. "There are heaps more. I haven't read them all—"

"That message doesn't mean Dad's having an affair!" I scoffed, while secretly beginning to wonder if it could *possibly* be true.

"Well it would explain why Mum's kicking him

out, wouldn't it?" Gemma demanded.

"Mum *isn't* kicking him out!" I screamed at her.

"Well, they're separating, aren't they?" Gemma shot back, giving me a shove. "People don't just split up for nothing!"

I knew, logically, that Gemma was just as unhappy, confused and frustrated as I was, but that didn't stop me from shoving her back. Gemma stumbled slightly and almost stepped on Lewis's paw. He jumped out of the way and began to bark his head off.

"Now look what you made me do!" Gemma scowled at me. "It isn't *my* fault that Dad's got a girlfriend—"

"You don't know that for *sure*!" I shouted.

"Well, where is he *now*, then?" Gemma shrieked at the top of her voice. "Look at the time, Grace! Staff meetings at school don't go on this long! I'm telling you, Dad's having an affair and that's why they're getting a divorce—"

Suddenly the front door swung open. Gemma and I were so shocked we almost fell over. We turned to see Mum and Dad standing outside staring at us. We'd been making so much noise, we hadn't heard the key in the lock.

"Hello, girls," Mum said quietly as Lewis, tail wagging, went over to greet them. I shot a quick glance at Gemma. She'd been red in the face, but was now pale, and she was probably wondering, like me, how much Mum and Dad had heard.

"I think we'd better go into the living-room and have a chat," said Dad. He looked tired and strained as he put his heavy bag of books and papers down on the hall table. Then he reached for the phone I was still clutching. "I'll take that, Gracie."

We all filed into the living-room and sat down in silence. No one seemed to want to start the conversation, which wasn't surprising as I had a gut feeling it wasn't going to be very pleasant for any of us. All I wanted to know was if what Gemma had said was true.

"Right, I think we need to talk." Mum cleared her throat and then glanced enquiringly at Dad. He nodded.

"I do *not* have a girlfriend," he said with emphasis, looking from me to Gemma. "That isn't why your mum and I are separating, girls. I'm late home because your mum's car broke down and I had to go and collect her from the gym."

"But those messages!" Gemma burst out.

"Lilly Bennett is my solicitor, Gem," Dad said gently, and I felt my whole body sag with relief.

"Funny kind of messages to get from your solicitor," Gemma muttered mutinously.

"I've known her for a while," Dad explained. "She's Bryan's sister." Bryan was one of Dad's friends and colleagues at school, the one he'd said he was going to move in with.

I cast a hostile glance at Gemma. *She* was the one who'd jumped to conclusions and been so ready to think the worst of Dad. I was *so* relieved that had been cleared up.

"But *why* do you need a solicitor, Dad?" Gemma demanded, still bristling with anger. "Is there something you and Mum aren't telling us? Have you secretly been planning to get divorced all along?"

"No, we haven't, Gemma," Dad replied firmly. "We told you, this is just a trial separation. Your mum and I are keeping an open mind about the future—"

"Yeah, *right*," Gemma broke in scornfully.

I glared at her. This painful scene was all Gemma's fault.

"You shouldn't have been sneaking around looking at Dad's phone, Gemma!" I burst out.

"Oh, shut up!" Gemma shrieked. "Don't tell me what to do!"

"Girls, *please*." Mum's voice broke. "You two are the most important people in all this, and your dad and I just want to figure out the best way forward from here for all of us."

Dad sat on the sofa and slid his arm around me. "Everything we're doing is with you in mind, girls," he said, his voice full of emotion. "We just want to spare you as much pain as possible."

"Well, why don't you just stay together, then?" I blurted out.

Mum and Dad shared a distressed glance. I gulped, trying not to cry. I was *so* sick of crying.

"We're trying to decide whether that's the best thing or not, Gracie," Dad said after a long, tense silence. "It doesn't make any difference to the way we feel about you two. But at the moment your mum and I need some space from each other. We just can't live together for a while."

"What you really mean is you might *never* get back together," Gemma insisted miserably. "So why don't you just say it? You *are* going to get divorced, aren't you?"

"Like I said, sweetheart, your mum and I haven't

decided what we're going to do yet," Dad replied in a quiet voice. "But believe me, girls, divorce is a decision we won't be taking lightly."

I tried to say something, but the lump in my throat was too huge. I was trying to get my head around the fact that at half-term, Dad would be moving out and maybe never coming back. Everything would be horribly different, and there was nothing I could do about it. Gemma's shoulders were slumped now, too, and she sat there looking defeated, even when Dad got up to hug her.

"Maybe I should move out right now," Dad said heavily, turning to glance at Mum. "It might be less disruptive—"

"NO!" Gemma and I gasped. While Dad was here, there was still a faint hope that they *might* change their minds and maybe he wouldn't have to move out. I was *so* relieved when Mum shook her head.

"Let's stick to what we agreed, Will," Mum said unhappily. "Now, I'd better start dinner."

Dad followed Mum out and I could hear them talking quietly as they went to the kitchen, although not what they were saying. I almost smiled. It was *ridiculous* – Mum and Dad seemed to be getting on better than ever now they'd decided to split up and everything was out in the open. They hadn't had a single argument since Saturday, as far as I knew. It was Gemma and me who were at each other's throats.

"This is all wrong," Gemma muttered.

"I know, but *don't* try to blame everything on Dad," I warned her.

Gemma looked at me with dislike and then flounced out of the room. I sighed. Maybe mine and Gemma's relationship would have become difficult anyway, without the added pressure of Mum and Dad splitting. She obviously felt the need to – how had Lauren put it? – *step out of my shadow*. But her attitude was making life at home a whole lot worse.

Secretly I was also beginning to wonder what would happen if Mum and Dad *didn't* get back together. To be honest, I didn't know who I wanted to live with, and having to make a decision would tear me apart. But I couldn't bear to think of Dad living all alone somewhere. He'd get his own place, and then I could move in with him if I wanted to. But could I *really* leave Mum and Gemma?

Lewis rested his cold nose gently on my hand, and I patted his head as another thought struck me. Would Dad take Lewis with him when he left? After all, he was the one who'd bought Lewis when he was just a puppy. Mum hadn't wanted a dog at the time, although now she loved Lewis as much as the rest of us did.

I rested my head on the back of the sofa and closed my eyes. My mind was just crammed absolutely full with thoughts and fears and worries, and it felt like it was going to explode. I smiled bitterly as I thought back to the beginning of the season when Georgie had got so down and depressed after Freya Reynolds, our previous coach, had left, very unexpectedly, to be replaced by Ria Jones. I'd given Georgie several lectures about how change could often be a good thing.

But now my life was changing in ways I'd never even dreamed of, and I didn't like it one little bit...

"*Concentrate*, Grace!" I murmured to myself. I fixed my gaze firmly on Katy and a couple of the other Stars defenders, Jo-Jo and Debs, who were battling with the Swallows' strikers for the ball. "Don't lose sight of the action for a *minute*."

Another Saturday, another football match – an away game against the Shawcross Swallows. The Swallows had been beaten by the Blackbridge Belles last week and they were four places below us in the league, but this wasn't turning out to be an easy game for us. The Swallows seemed determined to get their bid for promotion back on track, and for the last ten minutes they'd been continually hassling and hustling their way down the pitch to our goal. Somehow we'd managed to keep them from scoring by mass defending, and I'd been forced to go back and help out, too. The first half had ended 0-0, and we were now well into the second half. Ria was pacing up and down on the touchline, beginning to look a little anxious.

"I wonder if the Belles are winning *their* game?" Jasmin panted, running up to me as the Swallows' goalkeeper placed the ball for a free kick.

I shrugged. "Who knows?" I replied, but then realised from the look of surprise on Jasmin's face that I'd probably sounded a bit too casual. "I hope not," I added quickly. But, to be honest, that was the *last* thing on my mind at the moment. I'd only turned up today because I didn't want to let the other girls down, and it had been a real effort to make it to Thursday night training. I hadn't gone to our usual pre-match meet-up in the park on Friday night either, saying I was going out with my family (what a joke – what family?). My legs were like lead at the moment, and I felt as if I was carrying the weight of the world on my shoulders.

"Grace, you kind of look like you're not really here," Jasmin said anxiously, staring hard at me. Lauren and Hannah, who were nearby, heard her and turned to look at me, too.

"So what am I, then?" I replied, forcing a smile. "A hologram or something? Look out, the goalie's taking the free kick."

Hannah, Jasmin and Lauren immediately glanced up the field, and I was relieved that they'd switched their attention away from me. I didn't want them to know that Jasmin had hit the nail right on the head. I *didn't* feel like I was really there at all. I felt disconnected from everything that was happening around me, and that was why I was constantly having to remind myself to *concentrate*.

Meanwhile, the ball sailed through the air and landed right at the feet of a Swallows midfielder. She stared down at it for a moment, almost unable to believe her luck, and then she charged forward towards our area, exchanging swift, accurate passes with a couple of her team-mates. Our left-back, Debs, tried to tackle for the ball, but missed.

"Oops!" Lauren groaned, sprinting off towards our goalmouth, where Georgie was looking very worried at the onslaught of Swallows' shirts. "Here we go again!"

Jasmin and Hannah shot off after her. I followed, but at a slower pace. It wasn't that I didn't care if the Swallows scored, you do know that, don't you? It was just that, as the main striker, I wasn't supposed to go too deep, in case the break was on. That was what I kept telling myself, anyway.

There was a fierce scramble for the ball in our goalmouth. Georgie was wrong-footed by one of the Swallows' front girls, and Katy had to dive in and come to the rescue. She booted the ball out of our area, and it curved in a high arc, heading towards the middle of the pitch where I was standing. It was tempting to run back to collect it, but I held my position because I could see that Hannah was going to get to it first, before any of the Swallows.

She did, and immediately pushed it sideways to Ruby. Ruby to Alicia. Back to Ruby, to Lauren and then to ME.

"Don't mess up, Grace!" I warned myself silently as I raced forward with the ball at my feet. We'd worked our way closer to the Swallows' penalty area with all those passes, and we were in with a chance of a shot. *"Concentrate!"*

I glanced up quickly. Should I try to pass to Lauren, who was in the middle of the penalty area, but marked by a Swallows' player, or to Ruby, who was clear, but further out on the left? Or should I go for the shot myself?

When I had my football head on, I was used to making quick, clear decisions. I didn't have to think about it. But this time I hesitated. A tall, lanky Swallows defender was bearing right down on me and I utterly panicked, a feeling I'd never experienced on the football field ever before. My mind went blank and I froze.

Just before the defender reached me, though, the ball was whipped off my toes by Hannah. She swept the ball over to Ruby who sent a cross flying into the Swallows' box. Katy was lurking there – where had *she* come from? I hadn't even seen her make the run – and she headed it straight into the net.

"We've done it!" Lauren let out a huge gasp of relief as she ran over to slap Katy on the back. "God, I thought we were *never* going to score!"

I felt completely embarrassed as I went over to congratulate Katy. If it hadn't been for Hannah's quick thinking, I'd have made a total fool of myself. Instinctively I did what I always did, whenever I played well or badly. I glanced anxiously over at my dad in the crowd.

But Dad wasn't looking at me. I don't think he'd even noticed that I'd almost messed up or that we'd scored. He was staring off into space, a sad expression on his face.

Swallowing down a large lump in my throat, I turned to Hannah who was standing next to me.

"Thanks, Han," I muttered. "Don't know what happened to me just then."

"No worries," Hannah replied cheerfully, "we all have off days – even *you*, Grace!"

"Ha ha, very funny," I said, pretending to match her upbeat mood. But I couldn't see anything to celebrate, even when the ref blew the whistle to end the game just a few minutes later. Yes, we'd got the three points. But did I even *care*?

Georgie had raced down the pitch from her goal to join the rest of the team and they were all giving each other high fives. I realised that I'd better go and join in or I'd look like a complete party-pooper.

"Great stuff, Katy." I gave her a hug. "You saved the day right at the last minute."

Katy looked modest. "It was a team effort," she said, with a twinkle in her eyes. "Although I *was* great, wasn't I?"

"Get her!" Georgie jeered, slinging her arm around Katy's shoulders. "You did good, girl. But what about you, Grace? You were well off form today—"

"Here's Ria," Lauren interrupted diplomatically, throwing me an anxious glance. I was glad because although Georgie's frank comments wouldn't usually have bothered me, today I felt completely sensitive and vulnerable, as if I was going to burst into tears at any second. My emotions felt so raw and exposed that everything seemed almost too painful to bear.

"Don't do that to me again, girls." Ria grinned. "Good job I haven't got a weak heart!"

"What about the Belles?" Jasmin asked.

Ria groaned. "They won, too! But don't get disheartened, we still have that game in hand, and when we beat the Cats next Saturday, we'll cut the Belles' lead and pile on the pressure…"

As Ria led the others off to the away dressing-room, I hung back a little. I was finding it *so* hard to pretend that I was still as interested in the rivalry between the Belles and the Stars as the others were.

In fact, football had never seemed as trivial to me as it did today. Was it just because of what was happening with Mum and Dad? I wondered. Or maybe it was also that I was growing up and leaving my mates behind? I couldn't stop thoughts of the leisure centre boy popping into my head again...

"God, your team was lucky there, Grace!" Preeti Chopra, one of the Swallows players, came towards me as I trudged off the pitch. We'd been at primary school together so I knew her quite well. "I thought we had a point for sure."

"The Stars are a bit like Man U," I replied with a grin. "Never write us off until the final whistle blows! How're things with you?"

Preeti and I stood chatting for a few minutes, and I was glad to waste a bit more time before I had to go to the changing-room. The way I was feeling, the less I was around the others, the better. I was already feeling nervous about our usual Sunday get-together. I decided I'd just have to make a good excuse to get out of it.

After I'd said goodbye to Preeti, I wandered down to the changing-room. As I reached them, I heard Georgie's voice loud and clear, even though the door was closed.

"Well, she's obviously not playing her best, is she? What if she's like this against the Belles in a couple of weeks' time? We could end up losing the game."

I flushed. I knew Georgie was talking about me.

"Grace *does* look a bit tired at the moment," Katy said thoughtfully. "But it's half-term soon, so she'll be able to have a rest."

"Yeah, and if she *has* got problems, she'll tell us when she's good and ready," Jasmin chimed in.

"Grace knows how much we rely on her goals," Lauren added. "She's a good mate, she won't let us down."

I rubbed my eyes, feeling stressed and exhausted to the max. How *could* I explain to the girls that football had plummeted to the bottom of my list of priorities right now? I couldn't without telling them about Mum and Dad, and I didn't want to do that until I absolutely had to. Until there wasn't a single hope of Dad staying...

"Are we meeting up tomorrow?" Hannah asked. "Maybe then we can try to cheer Grace up."

"I can't." Jasmin's voice was muffled, and I guessed she was pulling something over her head. "We're going to visit my aunt and uncle."

"I can't, either," said Katy.

"Well, OK, let's leave it this week, then," Hannah replied. "I've still got a heap of homework to do before Monday, anyway."

I smiled with relief. I was safe, for tomorrow at least.

Right now, all I wanted was to be on my own.

I wandered through the park, keeping an eye on Lewis who was bounding across the grass, occasionally stopping to scrabble eagerly through piles of autumn leaves. It was a crisp, cold Sunday morning and the park was almost empty. There was no one around except people walking their dogs and the occasional jogger. That was the way I liked it.

Last night Mum had gone out with friends, and Dad had started packing, ready to move out. I'd stayed in my room, doing homework, and Gemma had gone to the cinema with some mates from school. My family was fragmenting and splintering and breaking up as we all began to lead separate lives. It was half-term soon, and I didn't think we'd be spending much time together.

Instead of doing my homework, though, I'd spent a lot of time lying on my bed, trying to figure out where everything had gone wrong. I thought that if

I could *just* pinpoint the moment when Mum and Dad had stopped being happy together, then maybe things could be fixed. But all I ended up with was a headache. If anyone had asked, I would have said that Gemma and I had had a happy, stable childhood. But maybe Mum and Dad hadn't been happy for years before this? It was like all those lovely family memories had been a complete lie.

Determined not to feel tearful yet again, I took a deep breath of cold, slightly frosty air. I was *sick* of crying. I didn't know it was possible for one person to have so many tears inside them.

I looked around for Lewis, and as I did so, I spotted a jogger in a black tracksuit in the distance. I saw him glance warily at Lewis and I smiled to myself. A lot of the dogs in the park thought it was great fun to chase after joggers and pretend to nip their heels, but Lewis wasn't like that. He was well-trained. He was snuffling around in yet another pile of leaves, and didn't even raise his head.

Wait a minute…

The jogger ran on, turning slightly to check where Lewis was. He didn't see me, but I saw HIM. Long dark hair, tall and slim – *OMG!*

You won't believe it.

It was THE BOY from the leisure centre, and now he was running away from me! How could I stop him?

"Lewis!" I hissed, my heart thumping with excitement. "After him! Go on, catch him!"

Looking puzzled, Lewis raised his head and stared at me with big dark eyes. I guess this wasn't a command he'd been taught at dog-training classes!

"*Lewis!*" I groaned. "You're not much of a Cupid, are you?"

I ran over to Lewis and clipped his lead onto his collar. When I looked up, the boy had vanished. I groaned even more loudly. I *had* to find him!

I raced off across the grass, Lewis scampering along beside me. He thought this was a great game and began barking his head off excitedly. We dashed around the café, which was closed at the moment, and then I stopped and stared around. The golf course was on one side of me, the children's play area on the other. But there was no sign of the boy. Where *had* he gone?

Then I saw him! He was now jogging across to the football pitches beyond the children's playground.

Pulling Lewis with me, I ran through the playground, weaving my way between the swings and the slides. The boy had started jogging around each of the football pitches in turn, so I could kind of guess where he was going to run next. Somehow I *had* to attract his attention.

Oh, brilliant idea alert!

I took Lewis's bouncy blue ball out of my pocket. Lewis wagged his tail expectantly, his eyes fixed on the ball in my hand. Then I waited until the boy began to run around the pitch closest to us. I hoped he might look over and notice us, but he had his head down as he pounded along

As the boy got nearer, I unclipped Lewis's lead.

"OK, Lewis, here goes!" I murmured, lifting my arm right back.

Then I flung the ball straight into the boy's path. My idea was that Lewis would go bounding over to him and the boy would stop, thinking the dog might be chasing him. Then we'd have the *perfect* opportunity to chat.

But it didn't turn out *quite* like that!

I watched as Lewis went careering after the ball. Suddenly I clapped my hand to my mouth in horror as I realised that I'd thrown it a bit too hard. The ball bounced once, twice, and then hit the boy smack on the knee. *Not so ace, Grace!*

"Ow!" the boy yelled, coming to a dead halt.

"Oh, God!" Feeling *totally* embarrassed, I raced across the grass. Lewis got to the boy first and, tail wagging, retrieved the ball. "I'm so sorry. I didn't mean to hit you!"

Frowning, the boy glanced at me. I saw his face change. Surprise, recognition – and then a gorgeous smile!

"Hey, that's OK. Don't worry about it," he said. "Er—" he hesitated, and I held my breath. "I think I saw you at the leisure centre last Sunday?"

"Yes!" I gasped, thrilled that he'd remembered me. "I saw you, too!" Then I could have kicked myself for being a bit too eager. *Play it cool, Gracie!* "Um – I mean, yes, I *think* I remember…"

The boy grinned at me (he had divine white teeth, and not a spot in sight – he was so *cute*!).

"So this mutt is yours, is he?" he asked, giving Lewis a pat. "What's his name?"

"Lewis," I replied, suddenly coming over all shy. "And I'm Grace."

"Nice to meet you, Grace. I'm Nathan. Should we shake hands or something?" His dark eyes twinkled at me.

God, my insides almost melted, and my heart

was fluttering like crazy!

"Which way are you walking?" Nathan looked at me enquiringly. "I'll come with you."

"Oh, *that* way." I pointed vaguely across the park. I intended to keep walking with Nathan for as long as I could, even if it took me and Lewis *right* away from the direction of home!

"So, do you go to the leisure centre a lot?" Nathan asked. I was glad he seemed confident and at ease and was able to keep the conversation going, because I was a nervous, excited wreck!

"Not really," I replied. "It's a bit expensive. Sometimes we go to the local pool, you know, the one in town."

"You're a good swimmer." Nathan looked sideways at me, but I was too shy to meet his gaze. "I was watching you last week."

"My dad taught me," I told him. "He teaches PE and French at Bramfield Boys' School."

"Which school do you go to?" said Nathan. "I'm at Blackbridge Community College..."

A few minutes later we were chatting easily and I was feeling less and less shy. Nathan and I liked *loads* of the same things which *has* to be a good sign, don't you think? We both loved swimming and tennis and hiking and holidays abroad and watching sport on TV. We both hated broccoli and soaps (except for *Hollyoaks*!) and drama lessons at school. But there was one thing I still hadn't mentioned...

"Er – do you like football?" I asked casually as Lewis began digging through an enormous pile of leaves. Don't be mad at me! I know it's completely girlie and stupid, but I *just* wanted to make sure that Nathan (or Nat, as he'd told me to call him) didn't think that girls' footie was a joke...

Nat laughed. "I like it, but I'm just no good at it!" he confessed. "My younger sister got all the football talent in our family, would you believe?"

"Oh, so your sister plays?" I tried not to sound too relieved. Nat obviously didn't mind about girls playing footie. *Result!* "So do I, actually."

"Really?" Nat didn't look taken aback, and I smiled. What had I been worrying about? "Which team do you play for? Maybe you know my sister."

"What's her name?" I asked curiously.

"Jacintha," Nat replied. "She plays for the Blackbridge Belles."

"*What!*" I shrieked, utterly horrified.

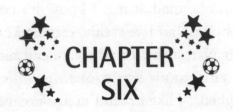

CHAPTER SIX

I simply could not *believe* it. Of all the boys in the world, I had to fall for the the brother of JACINTHA EDWARDS, the Blackbridge Belles' captain! I bit my lip, imagining what the others would say if they knew. Especially Georgie. I could almost hear her giving me earache, what with the important match against the Belles coming up...

Nat was looking bewildered. "Was it something I said?"

"No," I replied with an effort, attempting to force a smile. I was trying to remember if I'd ever seen Nat at any of our games against the Belles, but I was sure I hadn't. "It's fine."

"Come on, Grace," Nat persisted. "What's up?"

I sighed. I might as well confess, because it was bound to come out one way or another. "Has Jacintha ever mentioned a team called the Springhill Stars?"

"Has she!" Nat rolled his eyes. "They're the Belles' biggest rivals, aren't they? Jacks keeps going on about the match that's coming up and saying the Belles *have* to win. I'm pretty sick of hearing about it, to be honest—" He stopped abruptly. "You don't play for the Stars, do you?"

I nodded.

"So you're Grace Kennedy!" Nat exclaimed. "Jacky's always moaning about what a good striker you are."

"Thanks," I said glumly. My mind was in a spin. I desperately wanted to get to know Nathan – if *he* wanted to, that is – but I knew the other girls would think I was being a terrible traitor.

To my surprise, Nat burst out laughing.

"Of all the girls in all the world, I had to meet a Springhill Stars player!"

This was *so* like what I'd thought earlier myself,

that I couldn't help smiling.

"You're not bothered about it, are you?" Nat asked. "We can still be friends." He looked at me a little anxiously. "Can't we?"

"Oh, *yes*!" I said eagerly. "It's just that – well, I don't know if my team-mates will be too pleased."

"Does it matter?" Nat wanted to know. I thought about it for a moment. No, it *didn't* matter, did it? Why should it? I mean, I was *definitely* beginning to realise that football wasn't the most important thing in my life any more. Anyway, I'd still play my best against the Blackbridge Belles (even if my best wasn't THAT great at the moment, what with everything going on at home).

Once again I wondered if I was feeling like this because I was growing up and growing away from football, and my mates. It was *so* sad, but I couldn't help it. Football had been a huge part of my life up until now, but all of a sudden, I seemed to be ready for other, more adult things. And yet I didn't want to lose the five best friends I'd ever had...

"Hey, don't look so down, Grace." Nat touched me lightly on the arm. "We don't have to tell anyone we're mates, and I won't say anything to Jacintha. I haven't been to watch her play for ages, anyway."

He grinned at me, his dark fringe flopping into his eyes. "Anyway, football's only a game!"

I couldn't help laughing. *Try telling Georgie that!*

"It can be our secret," Nat said, winking at me. Then he glanced at his watch. "Look, I've got to go, Grace. But I'll be at the leisure centre on Thursday evening. They're starting a swimming club there for people our age. Would you like to come with me?"

A date! Nat had asked me for a date! All flustered and pink, I nodded, trying not to look too eager.

"I'd love to," I said. A little voice at the back of my head was saying, *What about footie training on Thursday?* but I ignored it.

I wasn't going to lose out on this chance to get to know Nat better.

"Do the words *Blackbridge Belles* mean anything to you, Grace Kennedy?"

Georgie's tone was quite menacing! I glanced over at her and completely missed the pass that Hannah had just sent spinning towards me. We were coming to the end of Tuesday night training, and we were finishing off with a few fun drills. Katy, Hannah, Georgie, Lauren and myself were standing in a circle with Jasmin being Piggy-in-the-Middle and trying to intercept the ball as we pushed it around. Because I was staring at Georgie, Jasmin managed to pounce on the ball with a squeal of glee.

"You're Piggy, Hannah!" she yelled triumphantly.

Hannah groaned and swapped places with Jasmin. Meanwhile, Georgie was staring back at *me*, hands on hips. She was frowning.

"I said, what about the Blackbridge Belles, Grace?"

My heart was thudding so loudly, I was sure Lauren and Katy, who were standing either side of me, *must* be able to hear it. Had anyone found out about me and Nat?

"What about them?" I snapped. My tone was sharp, and I regretted it immediately as the others, including Georgie, looked surprised.

"Well, you don't seem that interested in the match these days," Georgie said bluntly. "Is there something you're not telling us, Grace?"

I coloured right up. There were *two* things I wasn't telling them actually – one was Mum and Dad, and the other was Nathan. I felt horribly guilty as I saw the others exchange anxious glances.

"Sorry," I muttered.

"Is this about you and Gemma again?" Lauren

asked sympathetically. "You said you weren't getting on very well."

I nodded, glad to have been handed an easy escape route. "Yes, something like that," I agreed. It wasn't even a lie. Gemma and I hadn't really spoken since our row a week ago. She'd been all quiet and moody, and she'd hardly even said anything to Mum and Dad, either. She'd just stayed in her room or gone out with her mates. I knew that Mum and Dad were worried about her. "Just sister stuff."

"Tell me about it," Hannah said glumly. "Olivia and I had a big fight yesterday, and she threw a doughnut at me."

"Did it hit you?" Jasmin asked curiously.

"No, I caught it and ate it!" Hannah replied, looking so pleased with herself that we all laughed, even me. "It was the last one, so Olivia was *furious*, ha ha!"

As we completed the training session and Ria gathered us together for a final chat, I wondered if I should mention that I wouldn't be coming to training on Thursday. I couldn't say I was going to the swimming club though – and I hadn't really come up with a good excuse yet.

"Right, before you go, I want to let you know

that I'll be carrying on with training sessions during half-term next week," Ria told us. "I realise some of you will probably be going away with your families, though—"

"We're going to France the day school breaks up," Lauren chimed in, "but only for a long weekend. We'll be back on Tuesday."

"And we're going to Scotland," Hannah added. "We're back on Wednesday, so I'll miss this Saturday's game and Tuesday training."

Ria nodded. "I've already made sure we have replacements for you and Lauren this Saturday against the Kingswood Cats. A couple of the Stars under-twelves team are going to play for us as they don't have a match that day. Now, is there anyone else who won't be available this Saturday, or for the Belles game a week later?"

I listened in silence as Debs, Alicia and Ruby told Ria that they'd be away for some of half-term, too, although it looked like everyone would be back for the match against the Belles. I was secretly relieved, though, because I was realising that I'd have *loads* of free time during half-term next week to see Nat, especially if I skipped both training sessions. My absence wouldn't be so obvious with so many of the other girls missing. But I still had to come up with an excuse for missing *this* Thursday so I could go to the swimming club. I frowned slightly. I was beginning to realise just how much time playing footie had taken up over the years.

"Um – we *might* be going away during half-term for a few days, but we haven't decided anything yet," I said casually to Ria, just to cover myself. She nodded.

"OK, just let me know as soon as possible." Ria smiled at us all. "Now off you go. See you Thursday."

There was a chorus of "See you Thursday, Ria", and I joined in, but I felt like a bit of a traitor. How could I miss out on the chance of a date with Nat, though? You understand, don't you?

I followed the others to the changing-room, my mind working overtime. I was going to meet Nat this week on Thursday, and nothing would stop me. And I'd already decided not to go to either Tuesday or Thursday training during the half-term holiday next week, so that meant I'd be free to go to the second swimming club meeting – *if* Nat asked me again. It was something to look forward to, and believe me, I really needed it. At the moment the only thing I knew for sure was happening in the Kennedy household at half-term was that Dad was moving out and Gemma and I would almost certainly still not be speaking to each other. Nat was my escape from all the stress and misery. I wasn't sure what was going to happen to football, though, if Nat wanted to make our swimming club date a regular thing.

At some point I might need to make a very difficult decision.

"Grace, you'd better get ready if you're going to training tonight." Mum glanced at the clock as she and I loaded the dishwasher after dinner. It was Thursday, two days later. Dad was out with Bryan, and Gemma had eaten in silence, then gone to her friend Maddy's house. "Otherwise you'll be late."

"I was thinking of maybe not going tonight," I said as casually as I could.

Mum was so surprised she almost dropped the plate she was holding.

"Are you OK, Grace?" she asked anxiously. "You're not ill, are you?"

I shook my head, although this *was* the excuse I'd decided to give Ria and my team-mates. I'd kind of set it up at school today, mentioning to Hannah and Katy that I had a headache and felt tired. It wasn't a *lie*, either. As you can guess, I wasn't feeling my best with half-term – and my dad moving out – looming, although the prospect of seeing Nat again was making me fizz with excitement inside.

"I'm OK," I said quickly, "but I noticed that a swimming club is starting at the leisure centre tonight at six-thirty, and I'd like to go to that instead. Just for a change. It's a bit difficult being around the other girls at the moment…" I let my voice trail away, hoping that Mum would think I didn't want to go to footie training because I was finding it hard to hide my emotional upset from Hannah, Lauren and the others. Which was actually true, in a way.

"Well, all right," Mum agreed, still looking a bit surprised. I was glad it was her I was asking, though, and not Dad – he would *definitely* have tried to talk me into going to football. "I can drop you off on my way to work. But what about getting home? How long does the session last? You know my classes don't finish till nine-thirty."

"Oh, I'm not really sure," I replied vaguely. I didn't want to be collected on time in case Nathan wanted to go for a drink in the café afterwards or something. "I'll call Dad. Or I can get a bus home."

"OK," Mum agreed, "but if you get a bus, make sure you're home by nine, please, Grace, even if you have to leave the club early."

"Sure, Mum," I said. My heart was pounding fit to bust at the thought of seeing Nathan again. I hadn't been this excited since the Stars beat the Blackbridge Belles 4-1 three years ago! But I *was* only ten years old then. I'm a lot more grown-up now.

I ran upstairs, two steps at a time, to grab my swimming stuff. I'd already packed my pretty pink bikini decorated with crocheted white daisies, my hair brush, my make-up bag and the little bottle of posh perfume that my parents had given me last Christmas. I loved swimming, but all that chlorine in the water isn't exactly guaranteed to make you look and smell great, is it? And I *had* to look good afterwards in case Nat wanted to go to the café. *Note to self – do NOT have milkshake (very childish). Choose something more sophisticated instead!*

While I waited for Mum, I picked up my phone and sent the same text to Georgie, Hannah, Katy,

Jasmin and Lauren. *Sorry, guys, not feeling gr8. Think I'm getting a cold. Not coming 2 training 2nite xxx*

As I pressed the button to send the text, I felt incredibly guilty. Stop it, I told myself, that's just *so* typical of you, Grace Kennedy. Always doing what everyone else thinks you should, always trying to keep everybody happy.

Well, today, just for once, I was going to do what made *me* happy. But you've guessed it – I still felt guilty when I started receiving *Get well soon!* texts from the others. I soon cheered up when I arrived at the leisure centre and saw Nathan waiting for me outside, though.

So it was worth it. Wasn't it?

CHAPTER SEVEN

"Thanks for coming, Grace." Nathan's warm brown eyes stared into mine and my knees almost *collapsed*. He had this effect on me all the time. It was scary and exciting and it felt – well – *really* grown-up. "It was fun, wasn't it?"

"Yes, it was," I agreed. Things had gone even better than I thought because the organisers had divided us up into groups according to our swimming ability, and Nat and I had been in the same group. We'd had lots of opportunities to chat, and he was *brilliant* company. He was gorgeous, funny (in a good way!), interesting and talented.

The Perfect Prince, ha ha! And I was falling head-over-heels for him, although he hadn't so much as held my hand yet, which was a bit disappointing, to say the least.

"Shame you can't stay for a drink in the café," Nat went on as we strolled out of the leisure centre.

"I know," I sighed. It was *sooo* frustrating! When I'd gone to change after the swimming club finished at 8 pm, I'd had a text from Dad saying he was collecting Gemma from Maddy's and that he'd stop by the leisure centre around 9 pm to pick me up, too. I'd thought about sneakily texting back, saying I was already on the bus – just so that I could have a quick drink with Nathan – but I didn't have the nerve.

"And you're *definitely* coming next week?" Nat asked earnestly, looking like he *really* wanted me to say yes, which made my heart go pitter-patter!

I nodded. I'd worry about what to tell Ria and the others later.

"Cool." Nat winked at me. "Maybe I'll see you before then though? We could meet up in the park or something."

"Yes, please!" I said eagerly, then blushed. "I mean, thank you. I mean—" I was completely flustered and tying myself up into very embarrassing knots.

"OK, well, now we've got each other's numbers, it'll be easy to get in touch whenever we want." Nat smiled deep into my eyes. "Shall I wait with you till your dad comes?"

"Oh, no, I'll be fine," I said quickly. I didn't want anyone else to know about Nat. He was my very own delicious secret, the only thing helping me through all the difficult stuff at home at the moment.

Nat grinned at me. "Bye then, Grace."

"Bye."

I felt a teeny bit disappointed as Nat walked off. I was hoping he might have given me at least a kiss on the cheek – even though I'd probably have fainted with shock if he had! But then I was *really* glad he hadn't because literally seconds later Dad's blue Renault drew up at the kerb with Gemma in the passenger seat. Had they seen me and Nat together?

"Oh, hi!" I exclaimed, trying to sound bright and upbeat as I ran over to the car. I scanned their faces anxiously before I climbed into the back seat, but neither of them were looking surprised or curious.

"Hi, Gracie," said Dad. "Jump in, love."

I climbed into the back seat. I was glad that Nat had disappeared down a side road as Dad drove off. If Nat had spotted me and waved, I'd have had to explain who he was. My parents are pretty laid-back, but, as Nat didn't go to the same school as me and they'd never met him before, I was sure they'd want to know all about him.

"Did you have a good time, Grace?" Dad asked as we stopped at traffic lights.

"Fab," I replied enthusiastically. Of course, that was more to do with Nat than with the swimming club, I guess!

"I must admit, I was a bit surprised when your mum said you were missing football training," Dad remarked. "I don't think you've missed a session since you were about ten!"

I blushed, glad that it was dark and the interior of the car was dim. "Well, I just wanted to try something different, for a change," I murmured.

"Who was that boy you were chatting to just now?" Gemma interrupted curiously, turning in her seat to stare at me.

Oh, bum! I was taken by surprise, but I was determined not to react. However, I couldn't stop a wave of pink flooding into my face and making me feel all hot and bothered.

"Ooh, I think Grace is blushing!" Gemma observed with a smirk.

"Which boy?" Dad asked. "I didn't see anyone."

"He left before we stopped," Gemma told him helpfully. "I got a good look at him, though, because they were standing under the lights at the front of the leisure centre, and I didn't recognise him. Is he your boyfriend, Grace?"

"Don't be stupid!" I snapped, squirming in my seat and wishing I was a million miles away. "He's just a friend."

"Yeah, right," Gemma said in quite a sneery tone. "I suppose you think you're *so* great because you're first to get a boyfriend—"

"He is NOT my boyfriend!" I yelled. "What's your problem?" Oh, yes, I was doing a great job of not reacting! Trust Gemma to turn this into yet another competitive thing between us.

"Girls!" Dad said sternly. "That's enough."

I slumped down in my seat, biting my lip. This wasn't how I'd thought it would be when Gemma and I got interested in boys. I'd fondly imagined that we'd have lots of girly, giggly chats about the various boys we had our eye on. That obviously wasn't going to happen now that Gemma and I couldn't get along for five minutes without arguing bitterly. Once again, I wondered silently if maybe it would be best if I moved in with Dad, *if* he and Mum didn't sort things out and he ended up getting his own place. I was still hoping things wouldn't go that far. But if they did, it would give Gem and myself a breathing space that we definitely needed.

"Grace!"

I jumped slightly at the sound of Dad raising his voice.

"Sorry, Dad, I was miles away."

"Thinking about that boy, were you?" Gemma said immediately.

"Cut it out, Gemma," Dad warned. "I was just asking what his name is, Grace."

"Nathan Edwards," I muttered, wishing I could *kill* Gemma for starting all this.

"And he doesn't go to your school?" Dad probed.

"No, he's at Blackbridge Community College."

Dad didn't say anything else, and I was really relieved. Until we got home, that is. I'd gone straight up to my room to get away from Gemma and her sarky comments, really, but also because I had to read a bit of *A Midsummer Night's Dream* before English class tomorrow. I was lying in bed trying to read but thinking about Nat, when there was a tap at the door and Mum came in.

"All right, Gracie?"

"Yep," I said warily. Mum had a look on her face that I instantly recognised. It was what Gem and I had always called her *you're not going to like this but it's for your own good* look.

"Enjoy the swimming club?" Mum sat down on the edge of my bed.

I nodded, trying not to sigh with impatience. I could guess what was coming.

Mum hesitated. "You didn't tell me you were going with a friend."

"I didn't," I said, which, strictly speaking, was true. "I went on my own – *you* gave me a lift, remember?"

"But you knew this boy Nathan was going to be there?" Mum wasn't giving up and I just couldn't understand it. OK, my parents liked to know who I was hanging around with, but this was a bit much.

I thought about lying but I just couldn't. "Yes," I muttered.

"Have you known him long?"

"A week or two," I admitted reluctantly.

"Oh." Mum was silent for a few seconds. "Well, your dad and I would like to invite him round for tea during half-term," she said at last.

"*What!*" I shrieked.

"We want to meet him." Mum stared hard at me and I could tell she wasn't going to back down. But I wasn't going to give in without a fight, either.

"Oh, Mum!" I groaned. "It would just be the most embarrassing thing *ever*!"

For a moment or two I considered telling Mum that Nat was Jacintha Edwards' brother. After all, she and Dad had seen Nat's parents at our games against the Belles every so often, so it wasn't like they didn't know *something* about Nat's family. But I kept quiet. I think it was because I was afraid Gemma would use that information against me, somehow. In her present prickly mood, I could *just* see her deliberately blurting it all out to Georgie and the others when they came round here. So I didn't say anything.

"We only want to make sure he's the right kind of friend for you, Grace," Mum replied firmly.

I almost laughed as I finally realised what was going on. So *that* was why Mum and Dad were creating such a big fat fuss about meeting Nat. They were worried that all the stress and hassle at home might be sending me off the rails and making me fall in with the wrong crowd!

"You don't have to worry about me," I snapped. "Nat's very nice."

Mum ignored that. "Did you tell Ria and your mates that you were skipping training to go to the swimming club?" she asked.

My face flamed. "God, I'm sick of all these questions," I said sulkily. "I haven't done anything wrong!"

"I didn't say you had," Mum pointed out gently. "You must like Nathan a lot?"

I stayed stubbornly silent, but I guess my bright scarlet face gave me away.

"OK, well, invite him over for tea next Monday or Tuesday." Mum stood up. "We'll look forward to meeting him."

"You mean before Dad moves out on Wednesday?" I said sarcastically. "So we can pretend to play happy families?"

Mum sighed. "Good night, Gracie."

She went out. I rolled over and hid my face in my pillow. I wanted to *scream*. Why couldn't Mum and

Dad just leave me alone? They were already ruining my life by having this trial separation. But I knew that it'd be really difficult for me to see Nat now without Mum and Dad nagging me to meet him. And Gemma would be watching me all the time, too...

Sulkily I reached for my phone. At first I was going to call Nat, but I just thought it would be *too* embarrassing. So I decided to text instead.

Wd u like to come to my place 4 tea next week? G x

God, that took me *ages* to write. At first I was going to mention meeting my parents, but that sounded way too serious. I didn't want to put Nat off, and I just hoped he'd expect them to be here. I was also hoping that Gemma would be out. I didn't fancy having to put up with her teasing afterwards.

And what would Nat think about all this, I worried, as I pressed the 'send' button. Maybe he'd think it was all really childish and a big joke, and he wouldn't want to see me any more...

"Footie or picnic first?" Lauren demanded.

It was the following day and all our schools had finished at lunchtime because of half-term the following week. Texts had been flying backwards and forwards, and we'd arranged to meet in the park, bring a picnic for our lunch and have a kick-around. We always met up in the park on Fridays before a game, anyway, but usually in the early evening after school.

"Footie," Georgie said instantly.

"Oh, but I'm *sooo* hungry!" Jasmin wailed dramatically, dropping her bag on the grass.

"Lightweight," Georgie jeered. She tossed the ball she was carrying under her arm straight at Jasmin who shrieked as she caught it right in the middle of her tummy. We all giggled as we slung our bags down under a shady tree. God, I was feeling almost *happy* today after the stress of the last couple of weeks. Nothing had changed with Mum and Dad and Gemma, but school was over and the autumn sun was shining and it had been great to rush home after school finished early and get out of my uniform and into my jeans. Now I was chilling out with my mates and dreaming about seeing Nat when he came to tea on Monday.

I don't know why I was so worried and embarrassed – Nat was really nice about it! I got a text right back from him, saying he'd love to come and meet my mum and dad, and what time should he arrive. Bless, he's so *sweet*. And at least I had *something* to look forward to now, before Dad moved out on Wednesday.

"I'm glad you're feeling better, Grace." Hannah tucked her arm into mine and gave me a squeeze. "It wasn't the same without you at training last night."

"Thanks," I murmured, feeling *horribly* guilty.

"I have to be home by four." Lauren scooped the ball up with her toe and began trying to bounce it from knee to knee. She managed five in a row before dropping the ball. "We're leaving for France tonight."

"Ooh la la, oui, Mademoiselle!" Jasmin said in the worst French accent I'd ever heard. We all shrieked with laughter.

"We're going to Scotland tomorrow morning, really early," Hannah remarked, stopping the ball dead with the side of her foot. "I'll be dying to know the result of the Cats' game though, so somebody had better text me the *second* it finishes."

"Me, too," Lauren chimed in.

"It's gonna be an easy win for the Stars," Georgie predicted confidently, "3-0, and Grace gets another hat-trick!" She pounced on Hannah, booting the ball away from her.

I chased after the ball as it bounced across the pitch. Katy ran after me and for a moment or two we pushed and shoved each other, laughing, as we each tried to get to the ball first. I only stopped abruptly, allowing Katy to sweep the ball away from me, when a couple of boys wandered past. One of them had dark hair, and for a minute, my heart racing, I thought he was Nat. Well, there was a chance he might be in the park this afternoon, wasn't there? And I didn't want him to see me acting daft and being childish. I wanted to look all cool and glam and sophisticated, didn't I?

"I hope you're not going to give the ball away *that* easily when we play the Belles, Grace Kennedy!" Georgie yelled at me.

I stuck my tongue out at her without thinking and then hastily shut my mouth tight. I didn't want Nat, if he *was* somewhere about, to think I was just some silly little kid. I was kind of hoping I'd see him, even though it could be a bit tricky with the other girls around. But I knew Nat would probably guess that these were my Stars team-mates, and not let on that he knew me. I could trust him, and that gave me a lovely, warm feeling.

As the others charged after Katy, I rushed over

to my bag and whipped out my little mirror. My make-up was fine but my hair was already a bit windblown, so I found my brush and smoothed it out.

"Right, three against three, no goalies, anything goes," Georgie shouted. "Get your butt over here, Grace, and stop admiring yourself in the mirror!"

I popped the mirror back into my bag and adjusted my jeans a little lower on my hips. I was wearing a cut-off top in a shade of deep lilac, and I had my shades perched on top of my head. I hesitated. Should I take them off to play footie or not? It was definitely more glamorous to keep them on...

Suddenly I glanced up and saw the ball flying towards me. With a tiny scream, I dodged aside and it flew past me.

"Nearly got you!" Georgie called, "Come *on*, Grace, and stop messing about!"

I made an instant decision and left my sunnies on top of my head. Then I jogged over to the others at a slow pace, bringing the ball with me. After all, I didn't want to look all red and sweaty if Nat happened to go by, did I?

"Get you." Lauren nudged me in the ribs. "This

is like having a kick-around with Victoria Beckham."

"OK, Hannah, Grace and me against Jasmin, Lauren and Katy," Georgie ordered, booting the ball to me.

"Who died and made *you* the boss, missy?" Jasmin asked cheekily.

Georgie didn't answer. Instead she nicked the ball from me and booted it towards the nearest goal. It bounced a couple of times before rolling between the netless posts.

"GOAL!" Georgie roared triumphantly. "We're one-up already."

"Ooh, *so* not fair!" Katy complained. She and Hannah belted after the ball as it rolled away towards the path. Hannah got to it first and kicked it back to Georgie.

"And Georgie goes for number two!" Georgie chortled, sweeping towards the goal again.

"That sounds rather rude," Jasmin commented, sticking her leg out. Georgie promptly fell over it.

"Foul!" she shouted as Jasmin ran away with the ball.

"You said anything goes," Jasmin reminded her cheerfully. Then she gave a shriek as Georgie came whizzing up alongside and shoulder-charged her. Jasmin fell on top of the ball, and immediately Georgie leapt on top of *her*. Hannah, Katy and Lauren ran over to them, and I followed at a more dignified pace, keeping a sharp eye out all around me in case someone I knew just *happened* to walk by.

"Get off!" Jasmin squealed, hugging the ball to her like a rugby player. "It's mine! No – don't tickle me!"

Hannah and Georgie were attacking Jasmin's ribs, her weak spot, and making her laugh helplessly. Meanwhile, Katy and Lauren waded in to try and help out their team-mate.

"Get off me!" Jasmin giggled, tears of laughter running down her face. She tried to push Georgie and Hannah away but only ended up shoving Lauren, who landed on the grass on her backside.

"Hey, you idiot, I'm on *your* team!" Lauren spluttered. She grabbed one of Georgie's legs, trying to pull her away from Jasmin, and Katy did the same to Hannah. By now the five of them were laughing fit to bust, and I was smiling too as I watched them. But I didn't join in. I don't know why. Usually I would've piled in like the others, just for a laugh. I guess maybe I've grown up a lot over the last few weeks, I thought, gazing off into the distance...

"Are we boring you, Grace?" Georgie enquired in a mock-polite voice as she untangled her arms and legs from Lauren's.

"Don't be an idiot, Georgie," I replied quickly. The others looked a bit surprised and I wished I hadn't sounded quite so snappy. "I'm *fine*."

"You don't sound it," Lauren said frankly.

"Lauren's right." Katy stared at me with that direct gaze of hers. "What's going on, Grace?"

We were moving towards dangerous ground here. I had to head the girls off *somehow*.

"Nothing at all." I laughed lightly, my tone implying that they were being a bit childish and silly. "Like I said, I'm fine. Just because I don't want to roll around on the grass shrieking my head off doesn't mean there's anything *wrong* with me. I mean, I'm *thirteen* now, for God's sake..."

Oh no, I could see by the looks on the girls' faces that my clumsy attempt to deflect their attention had gone completely *wrong*. Jasmin, Lauren, Hannah and Katy were looking shocked and a bit miffed, while Georgie just burst out laughing.

"Come on, you lot, looks like we'd better go and sit down and eat," she said. "Poor old Granny Grace can't cope with us!"

I managed a smile, but it was a big effort. We wandered back to the tree where we'd left our bags, and I could see that, although the other girls were trying to act normally, there were a few sideways glances at me. I could tell from the looks on their faces that my behaviour was confusing them somewhat.

Well, it was confusing *me* too, I thought unhappily. Nothing I did these days seemed to be right. I felt as if I was caught between two different worlds and getting pulled in different directions. I'd had to grow up fast the last few weeks with everything happening at home. And now there was Nat.

But did that mean I had to move on and leave my footballing friends behind?

I was beginning to come to the conclusion that that was exactly what it *did* mean.

"Hi, Dad."

I wandered into the study at the back of our house. Dad was at the desk, surrounded by a sea of paperwork. My heart missed a beat as I realised that he was packing up his papers, ready to move out on Wednesday. But at the moment he was leafing through the contents of a large brown envelope that I'd seen arrive in the post that morning. He was concentrating so hard, I don't think he'd even heard me come in.

"Grace!" Dad was so shocked, he almost jumped right out of the chair. Immediately he began stuffing the papers he'd been studying out of sight into his briefcase, closing down the computer at the same time. He looked guilty too, I noted anxiously. "I didn't know you were back, love. Have a good time with the girls?"

I nodded. It was easier than trying to explain how things had changed for me over the last few weeks.

"Sorry for interrupting," I said, casting a curious glance at his briefcase.

"Oh, it was just work stuff," Dad said hastily.

I didn't believe that for a minute, and I started to feel worried. Surely there couldn't be any *more* bad news to come. But why had Dad looked so guilty? Maybe it was just because he was moving out.

"Where's Gem?" I asked, more for something to say than because I really wanted to know.

"She went into town with her mates after school finished," Dad replied.

As if on cue, the front door opened and then slammed shut. Next moment Dad and I heard Mum come out of the kitchen. Then there was a scream.

"*Gemma!* Oh, my God, what have you *done*?"

Dad and I took one look at each other, then we both dashed out into the hall. Mum was standing there, her eyes wide with shock.

Gemma stared defiantly at the three of us. Her long blonde hair, the exact image of mine, had gone. It had all been cut off.

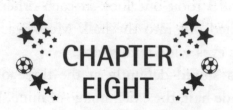

CHAPTER EIGHT

"God, what's the problem?" Gemma said in a totally bored voice. "I just decided to have my hair cut, that's all. I went into town to the hairdresser's with Maddy after school today and—"

"You could at least have *told* us," Mum said in a slightly shaky voice. I knew exactly how Mum felt. Gemma with short hair looked like a completely different person and it felt so *wrong*. I couldn't take my eyes off her.

"Asked permission, you mean?" Gemma said mutinously. "It's my hair, and I can do what I like with it!"

"There's no need to take that tone with your mother, young lady," Dad said in a stern voice. "You're thirteen, not thirty, and we'd just like to have known about it first, that's all—"

"Why are *you* sticking up for Mum, Dad?" Gemma demanded. "You don't even like each other at the moment! Anyway, Maddy suggested I get a tattoo as well, so just be grateful I didn't have *that* done—"

"That's enough, Gemma!" Mum snapped.

Gemma shut up, but she couldn't help running her fingers quite smugly through her wispy blonde crop. I was shocked as I began to realise that it *really* suited her. She looked older and more grown-up and sophisticated, all the things I was longing to be, and I felt quite envious. I wished I'd thought of having it done first.

"I just didn't want to look exactly the same as Grace any more," Gemma explained. "It's not a crime, is it?"

"What's wrong with looking like me?" I asked petulantly.

"Well, I don't now, do I?" Gemma said, trying not to sound too gleeful. She looked at Mum and Dad. "Look, I'm sorry I didn't tell you, but

I thought you might say no."

"I'm warning you, Gemma, if you ever do anything like this again without discussing it with me *and* your dad first, you'll be grounded for so long your hair will be down to your knees before you're allowed out," Mum said grimly.

"OK," Gemma said sunnily, not looking one bit bothered. She bounced upstairs humming to herself. Speechless, I watched her disappear into her bedroom and close the door. Quiet, shy Gemma who wouldn't say boo to a goose seemed to have completely vanished, and there was now a confident, outgoing teenager in her place. *And* she had a stunning new haircut that made me feel dowdy, frumpy and *childish*.

Mum was frowning. "Will, can we have a chat?" she said, ushering Dad into the study. I knew they were going to talk about Gemma. I also knew that the reason they hadn't come down harder on her was because they were worried about how she was reacting to their separation...

But what about me, I wanted to shout. What about MY problems? I was having to cope on my own, and because I wasn't going off the rails a bit, like Gemma, nobody seemed to care.

"God, this is the pits!" Georgie fumed under her breath as we all piled into the box for yet another Kingswood Cats corner. For once, I'd abandoned my striker's role and gone right back to our penalty area to help out. "They're running rings around us!"

"3-0 to us, you said, Georgie," Katy groaned. Her normally sleek dark hair was all messy and sticking up, and she looked more flustered than I'd ever seen her before. "I don't think we've even had *one* shot at goal so far!"

"This is about their millionth corner," Jasmin muttered, hopping agitatedly from one foot to the other. "But at least they haven't scored yet, either."

The Kingswood player took the corner and we all tensed. But luckily it was a really poor cross and it flew straight out of play. We breathed a collective sigh of relief. The Cats had come out fighting at the beginning of the first half, and they'd started the second half in exactly the same way. They were only a mid-table side with no hope of promotion, but they'd obviously decided to go for it. We couldn't even use the excuse that we were missing Hannah and Lauren, playing instead with two girls drafted in from the Stars' under-twelves team. Because the Cats were also missing at least *three* of their regular players, as far as I could tell.

"We need to get our heads down and work at it!" Georgie called fiercely as we dashed out for the goal kick.

I watched as she took a run-up to the ball, sliced it and it bounced out of play. Georgie looked furious with herself. Every single one of us was on edge because we knew getting these precious three points from a victory today would cut the Belles' lead at the top of the table dramatically – and I was even *more* on edge than the others. I'd been dreading this match, wondering if I'd be able to concentrate at all, but everyone else was playing badly too, so we were all in it together! No one had noticed that half my mind was on other things and although I knew it was mean, that made me feel loads better.

Katy and one of the Cats strikers were jostling for the ball. Katy lost it, but I saw her mouth set in a determined line as she went after the other girl and won the ball back. She pushed it forward to Jasmin, too hard, and it zipped past her to a Cats midfielder. Jasmin raced after the Cats player as she turned with the ball, but one of Jas's bootlaces was trailing and she tripped over it and went flying!

The Cats still had the ball and they were charging forward towards our goal like a pack of hungry wolves. This time Emily, Katy and Debs had to join forces to stop them. Desperately, Jo-Jo kicked the ball wildly away from our goal and by chance it fell right at my feet as I hovered on the edge of our penalty box.

"Go on, Grace!" I heard Georgie roar from behind me. "Run!"

The Cats had made the classic mistake of scenting victory on the horizon and had pushed everyone forward to try and get the elusive goal that they'd been pressing for. Although I was right down our end of the field, there was no one between me and their goal except for the Cats goalkeeper and two defenders.

I did as Georgie had said and ran, right into the Cats' half. I'd done this a million times before: raced towards the goal, taken on defenders and goalkeepers, dummied them, and scored from a variety of positions. I could do it in my sleep. So why, today of all days, couldn't I concentrate? Why did I feel like my brain was full of cotton wool and my legs full of lead? Where had all my enthusiasm for the game gone? As the first Cats defender came towards me, I made a weak attempt to take the ball past her. I knew it was weak and I knew it was bound to fail. It did. The defender hooked the ball neatly away from me and immediately passed it back to her goalie. I heard groans from the other Stars players and I felt *terrible*. Maybe I'd just lost us the game because that had been our one and only chance to score so far. *And* I'd be getting an ear-bashing from Georgie afterwards...

Suddenly, there were gasps from both sets of players and from the crowd. The Cats goalie had come out to collect the ball and had totally misjudged the force of the back pass. She tried to catch the ball on her chest as she wasn't allowed to handle it outside the penalty area, but she missed. The ball sailed past her and into the net. *Own goal!*

No one cheered or anything because we were far too sporting for that! But glancing around as the whistle blew, I could see the huge relief on my team-mates' faces. I was relieved beyond anything, too. I'd played terribly today, but I'd got away with it because everyone else was nervous too, and we didn't have our regular team. But I wouldn't be able to get away with it for ever. Sooner or later, my friends and team-mates were going to notice that my heart just wasn't in the game any more.

We were playing the Belles next Saturday, and what was going to happen then?

"Lauren says she knew we'd win!" Jasmin remarked, showing us the text on her phone as she, Katy, Georgie and I went into our favourite café, Mamma Mia's. Getting that goal had turned the match in our favour and, with the Cats really downhearted at conceding a goal after dominating the game, we'd managed to hang on until the very end. Georgie had suggested we go into town after the game to celebrate, and, although I didn't really feel like it, the others had persuaded me.

"Did you tell Lauren and Hannah we had to rely on an own goal?" Katy said with a grin.

"So what?" Jasmin beamed. "We got those three points, guys – and the Belles know we're coming right after them!"

The others whooped and started doing high-fives, but I pretended to be reading the menu on the wall. The pressure would only get worse before the Belles match, I knew. And it all seemed so *pointless*, really, considering what else was going on in my life right now... Anyway, whenever anyone mentioned the Belles, it made me think of Nat and then I started blushing so it was safest not to talk about it!

"I guess Lauren's swanning around the South of France looking like a celeb in her matching beachwear right now," I said, wanting to change the subject as we lined up at the counter with our trays.

"And Hannah's tramping the Highlands in her cagoule and wellies!" Georgie added. "The weather forecast said heavy rain in Scotland."

"Strawberry milkshake, please," Jasmin told the waitress. "Ooh, and a coconut macaroon, please."

"Are you keeping your strength up for the Belles match next Saturday, Jas?" Georgie teased.

Katy was hanging back a little, counting the coins in her purse carefully. We know better than to offer to buy a drink for her. She might not have much money, but she's very proud, our Katy. "Banana milkshake for me, please."

I hesitated. "I think I'll have a coffee."

Oh my God, what happened next was just toe-curlingly embarrassing! Georgie spun round to stare at me, and accidentally knocked Katy's purse out of her hands. Coins clattered to the floor and rolled *everywhere*. Meanwhile, Jasmin almost dropped her macaroon.

"*Coffee!*" Georgie repeated in an amazed voice, as if I'd just asked for a nice cup of poison. "What *are* you talking about, girl?"

"It's no big deal," I muttered defensively as we all got down on our knees and scrabbled around on the floor, picking up Katy's money. The others were starting to annoy me a little. It wasn't *my* fault I was growing up faster than they were, was it? "I just felt like a change, that's all."

"Did you bring your slippers and your knitting?" Georgie enquired as she collected her shake. Katy and Jasmin giggled.

"Oh, don't be so daft, Georgie," I snapped. "*Everyone* drinks coffee, not just *old* people!"

"Sure," Georgie agreed in a reasonable voice as we all went over to the cashier sitting at her till. "Hi." Georgie gave her a bright smile. "I was wondering, do you do discounts for OAPs?"

"Georgie!" I groaned, feeling embarrassed to the max. But I guessed that I was just going to have to put up with this kind of teasing from now on. I knew that as the others got older, too, that things would get easier, because we would all want to do more grown-up stuff.

But did I really want to wait that long? I wasn't sure that I did.

"So you met Grace in the park, Nathan?" Mum asked, handing round the tuna and cucumber sandwiches. She and Dad had been grilling Nat pretty relentlessly for the last ten minutes, ever since he'd arrived for tea this afternoon, and I was really worried he might run screaming from the house and never want to see me again!

Still, it had given me a bit of time to sit and catch my breath and try to stop my heart beating so fast. Nat looked so cute; I thought I was about to faint clean away when I saw him on the front doorstep! He was wearing a white shirt and black jeans and I just knew I blushed every time I looked at him. I was hoping Mum and Dad wouldn't notice. Of course, Gemma would have spotted it straightaway and teased me for the next ten years, but luckily, as I'd hoped, she'd gone out.

"Well, I'd seen Grace in the leisure centre the Sunday before," Nat replied politely. "That's why we got talking in the park."

I'd been really on edge in case Nat let slip that he was Jacintha Edwards' brother, but to my relief he hadn't. I mean, Mum and Dad wouldn't have cared, but they might have mentioned it to one of the other Springhill Stars' parents, and then it might have got back to my team-mates... I knew how Georgie and the others would react if they found out about Nat. They'd think I was a traitor. God, it was so *childish*, wasn't it? I really couldn't be bothered with it all at the moment.

"Do you enjoy sports then, Nathan?" Dad enquired. "Gracie's a fantastic footballer, aren't you, love?"

"Dad!" I muttered, embarrassed.

"Yeah, swimming, tennis and rugby, mostly," Nat replied. "I'm not much of a footballer. I like watching it, though."

Suddenly the front door opened and slammed shut, making us all jump. There was just time for my heart to sink like a stone before Gemma strolled into the room. I couldn't help glaring at her as she paused theatrically in the kitchen doorway.

"Oh, *hi*!" Gemma exclaimed, smiling at Nat. "You must be Grace's mystery boyfriend."

God, I could have *killed* her! Standing there with

her sophisticated new haircut, fluttering her eyelashes at Nat. I was speechless. This just wasn't the shy, quiet Gemma I'd known all my life – the one I'd grown up with.

"Hi." Startled, Nat glanced at her for a second, flicked his gaze to me and then back to Gemma. "I suppose you get this all the time, but you look exactly the same! Except for the hair, of course."

I sneaked a sideways glance and my tummy turned over with anxiety as I saw Nat staring admiringly at Gemma.

"Do you like it?" Gemma asked, beaming, running a hand through her crop. "I was fed up with looking like Grace all the time, to be honest."

"Well, Grace looks great." Nat turned to smile at me, but almost instantly his attention diverted back to Gemma. "But I can understand why you might want to look different as you get older."

Gemma grinned at him. She sauntered round the table and slipped easily into the empty chair the other side of Nat.

"I thought you were going out with Maddy," I said, trying not to sound too irritated. But as you can guess, I was!

Gemma shrugged, barely glancing at me.

"Maddy's mum decided to take her shopping," she replied casually. She reached for a sandwich and put it on a plate, then she leaned forward, closer to Nat, her chin on her hands. "So which school do you go to, Nat?"

God, I was absolutely *seething* with fury! I realised that she was actually *flirting*! With Nat – MY NAT! I sat there, trying not to choke on my sarnie, watching Gemma chatting with him and not being able to do anything about it. For the first half an hour, I did try to butt in and shut Gemma up a bit, and so did Mum and Dad, who must have realised what was going on. It was hard, though, because Nat *obviously* liked her, and *that* was really difficult for me to take. Gradually I stopped trying to join in the conversation, and the quieter I got, the more Gemma talked (or should I say, flirted). This wasn't what I'd expected at all. I had a horrible, sneaking feeling that now Nat had met Gemma, he preferred her to me, and I was *gutted*.

"You're not saying much, Grace," Nat commented at one point, turning to look at me while Gemma was in full flow, describing her most recent dance school production, *Bugsy Malone*.

"Oh, Grace has always been the quiet one,

haven't you, Grace?" Gemma interrupted with a mischievous twinkle in her eyes. I was gobsmacked! *What a cheek!*

When eventually Nat said he ought to leave, I was actually glad. I'd had enough of Gemma's behaviour by then. Mum and Dad were looking a bit concerned, too.

"Grace, why don't you see Nat out?" Mum suggested. Then, as Gemma pushed her chair back to stand up, she added quickly. "Gem, you can help me clear the table."

"OK," Gemma agreed cheerfully. She gave Nat a dazzling smile. "Maybe I'll see you again?"

"Maybe," Nat agreed, smiling back. Mum and Dad said goodbye, then gloomily, without a word, I led Nat out of the kitchen.

"Are you OK, Grace?" Nat asked as we went to the front door. "You were very quiet."

"Well, Gemma didn't let me get much of a word in, did she?" I said. OK, I know that was a bit bitchy – but it was *true*.

Nat laughed. "Yeah, talks a lot, doesn't she?" He winked at me. "It gets a bit annoying after a while!"

My heart soared. So Nat *didn't* prefer Gemma to

me! Everything was wonderful again!

"So, are you going to swimming club this Thursday?" I asked eagerly, opening the front door.

"I'm not sure." Nat frowned. "I've got a lot of stuff on. I'll text you, OK?"

I nodded.

"Maybe I'll see you around before then?" Nat suggested. "What are you doing Tuesday evening?"

"Nothing," I replied quickly, pushing all thoughts of footie training right out of my head. I'd already decided not to go – after all, some of the other girls were away with their families and wouldn't be going anyway, so I wouldn't be missed. I had to admit, it was weird feeling that football wasn't the be-all and end-all of everything, like it had been in the past. But I knew I'd *never* be able to explain it to my team-mates...

"All right, might see you around then. Bye, Grace." Nat grinned at me and left. I floated off down the hall on a cloud of happiness – until I got to the kitchen and found Gemma loading the dishwasher on her own.

"Nice try," I said, trying not to show I was still furious. "But it didn't work."

"I have absolutely no idea what you're talking

about, Grace," Gemma retorted coolly.

"Flirting and messing around with Nat like that."
I had to fight to keep my voice from shaking. "You
made an idiot of yourself."

Gemma smiled slightly. "*Nat* seemed to enjoy it."

"That's what *you* think," I snapped, "He said you
talked too much and it got on his nerves!"

I know, I know, that *was* bitchy, wasn't it? But
I was so *mad*.

Gemma's face darkened. "You've made that up!"
she yelled. "And I know why – you're just jealous!"
And, pushing me aside, she flounced out of the
kitchen.

I didn't go after her. Right now I disliked Gemma
so much, I almost *hated* her...

So it was turning out to be a fantastic half-term
holiday – *not*. Gemma and I weren't speaking at all.
Usually Mum and Dad would have tried to sort
things out between us, but Dad was busy finishing
off his packing. Mum was out a lot too, and I could
tell she was longing for Dad to leave, even though
she tried to hide it. That hurt.

It also hurt that Nat hadn't been in touch. I'd
skipped training on Tuesday, waiting for a text

about meeting up, but he hadn't contacted me. Then Wednesday started off really badly...

Dad was moving out at lunchtime, and he began taking stuff over to Bryan's house early in the morning. So this was *it*. Dad was leaving in a few hours, and if he and Mum didn't sort things out, he might *never* come back.

Gemma was locked away in her bedroom, not speaking to anyone. She didn't even come down to breakfast. Mum and I sat in the kitchen at the breakfast bar, pretending to eat porridge, but I just stirred mine round and round the bowl into a mushy mess. Mum ate a few spoonfuls and then pushed it aside.

"Right, I'd better go and call the family and let them know what's happening, now that your dad's leaving," she said quietly. She glanced at me. "Have you told your friends yet, Gracie?"

I shook my head. "I kept it secret because I was hoping—" I stopped abruptly, biting my lip. I couldn't get the words out. *Because I was hoping that you and Dad would sort something out, and he wouldn't have to leave.*

Now, remembering all the arguments and fights over the last year or two, I was rapidly losing *any* confidence that Mum and Dad would want to get back together ever again.

Mum stroked my hair. "Well, maybe you should tell your mates, if you feel up to it. It might help to have someone to talk to." Then she went off into the living-room to make the calls, closing the door behind her. Feeling completely down and depressed, I wondered how our grandparents, aunts and uncles would react.

Then, just to make me feel even worse, I got a text message. *Soz G can't make it to swim club thurs, Nat x*

I was *so* disappointed. Seeing Nat tomorrow had been the one bright spot in a very black, miserable couple of days. Now that wasn't going to happen. I might as well just go to footie training tomorrow evening after all, but the thought didn't cheer me up at all.

I heaved a huge sigh and sent a return text saying *OK* and signed with a kiss. At that moment the post rattled through the letterbox so I went into the hall, sorted Mum's letters from Dad's, and took Dad's into the study. I was bored out of my skull but I just couldn't seem to concentrate on anything much at the moment. I could spend a couple of hours on the computer surfing the net, I thought unenthusiastically, chucking Dad's letters onto a box of paperwork, which was waiting to be moved to his new home.

And that's when I realised. *Another* of those big brown envelopes, exactly like the one I'd seen before, had arrived in the post that morning. Curiously I picked the envelope up and studied it, remembering how Dad had looked that day just before half-term when I'd walked in on him. *Incredibly guilty*. What was going on?

I tried sliding my finger carefully under the flap to see if I could open it without tearing it. I didn't think twice about doing it (forget Golden Girl, Perfect Princess, goodie-goodie Grace – this was *important*). But the envelope was stuck fast. Then, as I reluctantly put it back with the other post, I noticed Dad's briefcase lying on the sofa. I went over to the briefcase and flipped it open. Then I began rooting through it as carefully as I could, looking for clues.

The briefcase was full of paperwork from estate agents about flats and houses for rent, some of it sent through the post and still in those big brown envelopes, other pages obviously printed off the internet. Dad had told us that he was looking for a place to rent so why had he looked so guilty about it? It didn't make sense...

And then something struck me.

"None of these places are in Melfield," I muttered, shocked, flipping through them again to check.

All the property details Dad had hidden away were for houses in Culverton, which was about fifty miles from Melfield. It was where Dad's parents, Nan and Grandpa lived, and where Dad grew up. His brothers and sisters and their families still lived there.

I suddenly felt so suffocated with fear, I could hardly breathe. It looked like Dad was secretly thinking about leaving us behind and moving back to Culverton. And if he and Mum couldn't work things out, then he probably planned to stay there.

Tears stung my eyes. How *could* he? He'd be *miles* away from Gem and me, and we'd probably only be able to see him during the school holidays and weekends, if we were lucky.

And *that's* when it hit me. Hadn't I been thinking for a while now that I'd prefer to live with Dad, and not with Mum and Gemma, if my parents didn't get back together? If I moved to Culverton with Dad, it would be a chance to reinvent myself and leave the old Grace Kennedy behind. Maybe Gemma and I would get along better, too, if we weren't living together. It would be a huge wrench to leave my mates, but I was beginning to feel that I was growing up and away from them, and from football, anyway. If I left with Dad, I could even stop playing football if I wanted to. Did I want to? I wasn't sure.

The thought of leaving Nat behind upset me, too. Maybe we could still see each other though, because I'd be coming to visit Mum and Gemma sometimes. And maybe Nat could come to Culverton to visit me.

I had to look at the bigger picture and I could see that this might be a *whole* new start for me, as well as for Dad.

If my family was going to split up anyway, maybe this was just what I needed!

CHAPTER NINE

"Don't let the ball touch the ground!" Georgie roared, lunging forward as Jasmin gave a squeal of dismay. To our surprise, Jasmin managed to catch the ball on her knee, and then lift it back over the net. She looked so surprised at her own skill, we all started laughing.

It was later on Wednesday afternoon, and we were playing football volleyball. No, I'd never heard of it, either! Lauren had arrived home from France the day before, and she'd texted us asking if we wanted to meet up in the park as she had a surprise for us. We'd all gone along, although we hadn't expected Hannah to join us as she'd only got back from Scotland a couple of hours ago. She did, though.

"You haven't got much of a tan, Han," Georgie remarked wickedly. "Ooh, I'm a poet!"

"What do you expect? It rained all the time we were in Scotland," Hannah groaned. "Gran gave Olivia a raincoat and a dodgy plastic hat to wear – she was *so* not impressed! Great that you beat the Cats last Saturday, by the way."

"We were rubbish, though," Georgie told her frankly.

"Must have been because Lauren and I weren't playing," Hannah said with a grin.

"Here's Lauren now," Jasmin chimed in. "And what on earth is she carrying?"

Lauren was struggling across the grass holding two long white poles, one in each hand, and she also had a roll of green netting tucked under her arm. She looked tanned and gorgeous.

"Going fishing, are we?" Georgie asked, running to give her a hand.

"Ha ha," Lauren retorted. "We played volleyball on the beach in France, so I thought us lot could have a go. My dad gave me a lift here."

"Did you have a good time?" Jasmin asked.

Lauren nodded, thrusting one of the poles at Georgie and the other at Katy. "It was fab, really warm and sunny."

"Don't mention the weather!" Hannah sighed, looking quite envious.

"Hang on a minute." Georgie was frowning. "I thought we were going to have a kick-around and prepare for the match on Saturday against the Belles? What's *volleyball* got to do with anything?"

"This is football volleyball!" Lauren explained with a wink. "Two teams, and we pass the ball over the net to each other *without* using our hands. So we're practising our footy skills. Get it?"

"Genius!" Hannah exclaimed. "Let's get this net set up."

Laughing and chatting, we chose a spot near the football pitches and then set everything up, pushing the poles into the ground and attaching the net to them. Well, everyone else was laughing and chatting. You might have noticed that I was very quiet. I didn't really know why I'd come, except that anything was better than being on my own at the moment.

My dad had finally moved out of the family home

a couple of hours ago. Trying not to show how upset I was, I'd helped him load the last few boxes into his car. Mum had said goodbye to Dad very quickly and then disappeared. I knew she was giving me and Gemma a chance to say our goodbyes properly, but Gemma wasn't even there. She'd said a brief farewell to Dad earlier and then gone out with a friend. Maybe she couldn't face the finality of it all, but it would have been great to have her around for support.

So it was just me and Dad standing there on the driveway with Lewis. Lewis was staying with us for the moment. Dad patted his head, then pulled me into his arms.

"This wasn't how I wanted it to be, Gracie," he murmured against my hair. "But there's no other way, unfortunately."

I swallowed down my tears. There was something I *had* to know.

"Dad, be honest," I said, my voice shaking uncontrollably. "How likely do you think it is that you and Mum will try again, and you'll move back home?"

Dad looked very troubled and my heart plummeted.

"I don't know, Gracie."

There was silence for a few moments. Although I didn't want to face it, I knew at that moment that the chances of my parents getting back together and not eventually divorcing were very small. I had to swallow several times before I could speak.

"How long are you staying with Bryan?" I asked.

"Not for long." Dad gave me a last squeeze and turned away to unlock the car. I couldn't see his face. "He doesn't have a lot of room. But finding the right place to rent is a bit difficult..."

My heart missed a beat.

"Have you decided where you're going to live yet?" I tried to sound casual. I didn't want Dad to guess I'd been poking around in his papers.

Dad shook his head. "I'm not sure," he replied evasively.

Was that true? Dad only had property details for Culverton, and none for Melfield, so that had to mean he was planning on moving away. Didn't it? Maybe Dad was going to commute to his job in Melfield for the moment, or perhaps he was going to look for a teaching job in Culverton, too, and make a whole new life there. Dad probably didn't want to tell me and Gemma yet because he knew we'd be upset.

As Hannah headed the ball over the net to Lauren, a horrible memory flashed into my head of Dad leaving, driving his car off the curb and disappearing down the road. I'd stood there with Lewis, watching until his car turned the corner, knowing that my old, happy life had just come to a full-stop, right there.

Lauren scissor-kicked the ball back over the net and it flew straight towards me. But I was frozen to the spot with misery and I couldn't have done anything with the ball even if I'd tried. It sailed over my head and bounced away, and I burst into tears.

"*Grace!*" Katy, who was on my team, immediately rushed over and flung her arms around me. "What's wrong?"

I was sobbing so hard now I couldn't see, but I was aware of the other girls crowding supportively around me. Someone – Jasmin, I think – handed me a crumpled but clean pink tissue.

"Grace, what is it?" Georgie asked urgently.

"My – my mum and dad have split up!" I wailed, hiccupping and gulping like a little kid. "They *said* it's just a trial separation, but I think they're going to get a divorce."

There was a shocked silence.

"How long have you known?" Jasmin asked, rubbing my back sympathetically.

"For a few weeks," I sobbed. "I didn't want to say anything before, in case they changed their minds..."

"So that's why you've been really down!" Lauren exclaimed, patting my arm. "I'm so sorry, Grace."

"We knew something was up," said Georgie. "You just haven't been your usual self, especially at football."

I dabbed my eyes with the tissue. "Football's been the last thing on my mind," I admitted.

I saw Georgie look alarmed. She opened her mouth to say something, but closed it again when Hannah shot her a warning glance. The others were looking anxious too, and I felt a surge of irritation. Were they really worried about me – or about the goals I was supposed to get against the Belles? Maybe I was being a bit unfair, but right now I just didn't care. I was sick and tired of worrying about how everyone else felt. It was a bit selfish, but I just wanted to think about myself right now.

"I know it's horrible, Grace, but you'll still see your dad all the time, won't you?" Lauren asked. "Are you and Gemma staying with your mum or might you go and live with your dad?"

"I don't know," I confided, getting a bit tearful again. "I'm pretty sure Dad's thinking of moving back to Culverton where my grandparents, uncles and aunts live."

"So you'll be staying in Melfield with your mum, then?" Jasmin wasn't really asking a question, more stating a fact.

I hesitated. I could tell a lie, but maybe it was better to start being a bit more honest.

"I'm not sure," I said finally. "I've been thinking of moving in with my dad, if they don't get back together."

There was a stunned silence.

"Grace, you *can't* leave Melfield!" Georgie gasped. "What about the Stars— OW!"

My eyes were too red and swollen to see much, but I guessed either Katy or Jasmin, who were standing either side of Georgie, had stepped on her toe or elbowed her in the ribs or something.

"Don't go, Grace," Hannah begged. "We'd miss you like crazy."

"You'd miss my goals, you mean." I hadn't meant to sound so snappy, but it just came out that way.

"That's not very fair, Grace," Jasmin said, looking a bit tearful herself now. "We'd miss *everything* about you."

"Look, I don't even know if I *want* to play football any more." Words came bursting out of me in a flood I couldn't control. "I just feel like I'm growing up, and I want to do different kinds of things. I'm not a little kid any more..." My voice trailed away. I still had *one* secret I couldn't tell them yet. *Nat*.

"What things?" Georgie demanded aggressively, but underneath her ferocious frown, I could see she looked hurt. The others looked upset and confused, too. That made me feel terrible.

"So you think we're childish to care about the Stars, Grace?" Lauren asked a little sharply.

I shook my head, but wasn't that *exactly* how I did feel right now? So it wasn't surprising the other girls looked unconvinced. Whatever they said, I knew they were worrying about how I was going to play against the Belles this Saturday.

"Shall we go and have a drink in the café or get an ice cream or something?" Katy suggested quietly.

"Then we can sit and talk, if Grace wants to."

"No, I'm fine." I dried my face and forced a weak smile, wishing I hadn't come and that I'd stayed at home to wallow in my misery. "Let's carry on with the game. I'd rather be doing something."

The ball had rolled away across the grass so Jasmin trudged off to retrieve it. Meanwhile, we all shuffled back to our team positions on both sides of the net. No one said anything, and everyone looked depressed. Georgie was still frowning angrily, but I knew underneath it all she was probably even more upset than the others. The Stars had been mega-important to her ever since her mum died, and she just wouldn't be able to understand the change in my attitude. I hardly understood it myself.

Jasmin came running back to us, the ball tucked under her arm, eyes wide.

"It's the Blackbridge Belles!" she gasped, pointing over at the children's playground. "Well, some of them, anyway."

A group of five girls were wandering through the playground towards us. One of them stood head and shoulders above the others.

"Lucy Grimshaw!" Georgie groaned, pulling a face.

"Who are the others?" Katy asked, screwing up her eyes to try and see.

"That's Chloe Parker and Alex Lowrie next to Lucy," Hannah replied. "I can't see the other two."

My heart was thudding really uncomfortably as I tried to make out the identity of the other girls half-hidden behind Lucy. As you can guess, there was no way I wanted to meet Jacintha Edwards. If she mentioned Nat, I'd *definitely* go bright red.

"I think the others are Kellie Burns and Sonia Ali," Lauren said.

My knees sagged with relief. No Jacintha, then, thank God!

The Belles were giggling and whispering to each other as they got closer to us. I was struck yet again by how TALL Lucy Grimshaw was. Georgie, Hannah and I were quite tall ourselves, but Lucy towered over us like a skyscraper!

"So you've given up on football then, Stars?" Lucy chuckled, pointing to the volleyball net. "Very sensible. We're going to whip your butts on Saturday!"

"Tee hee," Georgie retorted. "How amusing. Actually we're practising our already outstanding football skills by not using our hands." She took the ball from Jasmin, tossed it up into the air and kicked it over the net. Katy headed it back and Lauren caught it on her chest and then knocked it to Jasmin. It was a bit high, though. Jasmin made a valiant attempt to leap up to head the ball, but missed. She lost her balance as she landed, stumbled and crashed into the net, bringing that down with her as she fell.

All the Stars rushed to untangle her while the Belles fell about laughing.

"Yep, I see what you mean about those outstanding football skills!" Alex Lowrie giggled.

"Let us show you how it *should* be done," Sonia Ali chortled. She grabbed our ball and started bouncing it from knee to knee. She was *good*. After ten bounces, she caught the ball on her toe and passed it to Chloe. Immediately Georgie nipped between them and intercepted it. She scooped the ball up and chipped it to me.

"Go on, Grace," she yelled, "show them what you can do!"

I was taken by surprise, but I managed to catch the ball on top of my head and hold it steady there – the 'head stall', it's called! Then I tossed the ball upwards and when it dropped down behind me, I flicked it with the back of my heel to Katy without letting it touch the ground. The six of us had spent a day at a Brazilian soccer skills school for Lauren's birthday, and this was all stuff we'd learned there. Even though I didn't think football was so important any more, it still gave me a warm glow to be able to do those kinds of tricks.

The Belles were looking distinctly unimpressed though.

"Is that the best you can do?" Kellie Burns scoffed. "Give me that ball!"

"Ooh, this is just like one of those rap videos," Jasmin whispered to me as Kellie ran over to Katy. "You know, when they all show off their best dance moves!"

Katy allowed Kellie to get really close to her. Then, at the last moment, she pushed the ball neatly through Kellie's legs to Hannah. Hannah wasn't quite quick enough though, and Lucy nabbed the ball. She did a couple of Cristiano Ronaldo-style step-overs when Hannah tried to tackle her, and then scooped the ball up over Hannah's head to Chloe.

"Hey, you guys!" There was a shout from behind us. "I've been looking for you everywhere!"

Oh no! I recognised that voice!

I spun round, and there was Jacintha Edwards heading across the park towards us.

"Um – maybe we ought to go," I suggested quickly.

"Not till I get my ball back!" Georgie retorted. The Belles were knocking the ball around between themselves and wouldn't give it up, not until Katy slid in with a neat tackle and chipped it over to Georgie.

"I thought you said we were meeting in the playground," Jacintha grumbled as she joined Lucy and the others.

"Well, we saw the so-called Stars practising hard for Saturday, so we thought we'd better show them how the beautiful game is *really* played!" Lucy grinned.

Jacintha laughed. Then, for the first time, she seemed to notice me. Her gaze narrowed suspiciously and a thrill of horror ran down my spine.

"Oh, hi, Grace," Jacintha said. "Is it true that you're my brother's girlfriend?"

CHAPTER
TEN

Everyone, Stars and Belles alike, turned to stare at me in complete shock. And you've guessed it, I just couldn't stop myself from turning fire engine red.

"What's Jacintha talking about, Grace?" Jasmin asked, confused. "You don't have a boyfriend, do you?"

Now coloured scarlet, I shook my head mutely. Much as I wanted Nat to be my boyfriend, he wasn't *really*. Not yet, anyway.

"OK, then you're *very* good friends with my brother!" Jacintha persisted. "That's true, isn't it?"

"So what?" I mumbled, wishing hard I sounded

more confident that I did.

"You're mates with Jacintha's *brother*?" Lauren looked utterly taken aback. "You never mentioned it, Grace!"

"Why should I?" I snapped. "It's got nothing to do with the Stars, or football!"

"Of course it has!" Georgie shouted. I *knew* she'd react like this, I just knew it. "You can't be friends with the enemy!"

"Oh, grow up, why don't you!" I retorted. "I can be friends with anyone I like – football's only a game, anyway!"

Not so ace, Grace. BIG MISTAKE. Georgie looked like she was about to explode with rage.

"Oh dear." Jacintha smiled at the other Belles. "It seems the Stars have a *lot* of work to do to get their team back on track for Saturday!" And the six girls strolled away, arm-in-arm, laughing.

"You big traitor, Grace!" Georgie exclaimed.

"Georgie, be quiet!" Katy said in a voice more forceful than I'd ever heard before. "Remember, Grace is having a tough time at the moment."

"How long have you know Jacintha's brother, Grace?" Jasmin asked, looking distressed. "Longer than you've known *us*?"

I shook my head. "I met Nat a couple of weeks ago," I muttered. "It's no big deal."

"Is Nat the reason why you've been missing training?" Hannah asked slowly, "Like the time you said you were ill just before half-term?"

God, I just *wish* I could stop blushing – it's such a giveaway! I didn't answer Hannah's question, but I knew my face told its own story.

"So you fancy him then," Lauren concluded.

"Well..." I cleared my throat. "It's not exactly a crime, is it?"

"No, but does fancying some dopey boy mean you can't be interested in football, too?" Georgie said, looking distinctly unimpressed. "Does it mean you have to lie to your mates and think he's more important than *us*?"

I was shocked. "No!" I exclaimed. But wasn't that what I'd been doing? I started to feel guilty, but I wasn't going to go there, so I pushed the emotion aside. For once, this was about ME and what I wanted, no one else.

"Boys come and go, Grace," Hannah said quietly. "God, Olivia's had about three boyfriends in the last two months! They're not worth losing your mates, *or* the things you love doing for."

I bit my lip. I'd been feeling all grown-up and important and a bit superior to the others. So why did it feel like *they* were being more adult about this now than I was?

"I've got to go." And I was off, running across the park before anyone else could react. "See you."

I heard Katy and Lauren call after me, but I didn't stop. I ran across the football pitches, not looking round, until I was out of sight of the other girls. Still upset, I slowed down and took my phone out of my pocket. I needed to talk to someone.

Hi nat what u up 2? can we meet + talk?

A few seconds later a reply came buzzing back.

Sure, I'm in the park, where r u, at home?

My heart leapt and my face broke into a smile. Nat was already here, in the park! Quickly I texted him back and waited impatiently for a reply. Nat told me he'd love to see me, and that he was near the boating lake, right over the other side of the park.

I shoved my phone into my pocket and hurried off. It was a bit of a long walk to the lake from the football pitches, but I was glad. The other girls would never think to look for me there, as we didn't often go to that area of the park. They'd probably assumed I'd gone straight home.

I made my way to the boathouse, as Nat had told me to do, and then walked around the lake, avoiding crowds of hungry ducks looking hopefully for bread. Nat had said he was on a bench about two minutes walk from the boathouse... I squinted ahead of me in the pale sunshine, trying to spot him. I couldn't see him, though. But I DID see someone else.

"*Gemma!*" I gasped.

Gemma was sitting on a bench on her own, gazing over the lake. She almost fell *off* the bench though when she heard my voice.

"Grace! What the hell are you doing here?" she demanded. "Have you been following me?"

I stared at her in amazement. "Don't be stupid!" I snapped. "I came to the park with Katy, Georgie and the others. What are *you* doing here?"

Gemma hesitated. "I'm just with a friend," she mumbled sheepishly.

A terrible suspicion was beginning to dawn on me. "What friend?" I asked, hoping against hope that I was wrong.

Gemma stared defiantly at me. "Nat Edwards."

I couldn't believe it. "But – he's *my* friend!" I blurted out. "He's just asked me to meet him here."

"Well, he texted me an hour ago and asked if

I fancied a walk in the park with him," Gemma replied triumphantly. "He's just gone to buy us ice creams."

"He couldn't have texted you – he doesn't have your number," I said accusingly. "Did you steal his number from *my* phone and text *him*?"

"No, I didn't!" Gemma looked furious that I'd asked her that, but what was I supposed to think? "If you *must* know, Maddy's older brother, Josh, is in the same class at Blackbridge College, and he gave Nat my number." She sighed. "Look, Grace, I know this isn't easy for either of us, and I know you met Nat first, but I really like him, and I think he likes me—"

"No, he doesn't." I glared at her. "I told you, he said you talked too much!"

Gemma looked hurt. "Well, he told me you were boring," she retorted. "Grace is too much of a good little girl to be interesting, that's what he said!"

"I don't believe you!" I shot back. I couldn't understand why Nat had invited me to meet him while he was with Gemma. The only explanation I could think of was that Gemma had talked him into meeting up with her, and Nat wanted to make it clear that it was *me* he liked best, and not her.

"Oh, hi, Grace," a cheerful voice interrupted us. Which was lucky, because I think Gemma and I were about to throw each other in the lake. Nat was strolling towards us, holding two Cornettos. He handed one to Gemma and then he offered the other to me with that cute smile. "Here, take this, Grace, and I'll get another."

"No, I'm fine, thanks," I said quickly. Gemma was looking angry and I was all fired up too, and I didn't know *what* to think. But I wasn't going to give Nat up without a fight.

"Well, shall we *all* go for a walk, then?" Nat asked, glancing from me to Gemma. Gemma and I eyeballed each other sullenly and nodded. Just then there was a blast of ballet music, and Gemma began scrambling around in her bag for her phone.

"Oh, hi, Maddy," she said, throwing a suspicious glance at me and Nat as we moved aside slightly, "I can't really talk now."

"Sorry, Grace," Nat said under his breath as Gemma continued her conversation with her friend. "It'd be better if we were on our own, but there's nothing I can do. You know I like you best, but she's pretty persistent, your sister. She's been texting me all the time the last few days."

"Really?" I asked with a frown, wanting desperately to believe him.

Nat nodded. "That's why I was so relieved when you texted me just now. You've just saved my life! You will stay, won't you?"

"All right," I whispered back as Gemma cast yet another suspicious look our way. "It'd be great if we could be on our own, though."

"We'll meet up soon," Nat murmured. "Sorry I can't make swimming club tomorrow, but I'll text you." He slid his arm around my shoulders and gave me a quick squeeze. I couldn't help glancing at Gemma, and I saw her face darken. "Don't leave me alone with her, will you?" Nat went on with a rueful smile. "She's a bit full-on!"

"No, of course I won't," I promised. Gemma was making a fool of herself. Why couldn't she just accept that? It was me Nat was interested in, it was *so* obvious.

"Come on, girls, let's see your best shots," Ria called as we stood in front of the goal in single file. Katy and Georgie were standing on either side of the goalposts on the touchline, and we were supposed to run forward, pass to either Katy or Georgie, receive the pass back and then shoot for goal with our first touch.

"What am I doing here?" I asked myself silently as Jo-Jo dribbled forward, punted the ball to Katy, got a neat pass back and then skied the ball right over the crossbar. I'd thought about not turning up to training tonight, but it was our last session before the Belles match on Saturday, and however unsettled I was feeling, I couldn't let the other girls down. I *had* to play on Saturday. But I'd been hoping Nat would change his mind about going to swimming club, and if he'd asked me to go tonight – well, I would have said yes.

Things between me and Gemma were at an all time low. We'd walked around the park with Nat, each of us waiting very pointedly for the other to leave and neither of us wanting to be first to give in. In the end, though, it was Nat who'd had to leave, and when he'd gone, Gemma and I hadn't held back.

"You're making a real fool of yourself, Grace Kennedy!" Gemma had shouted angrily. "Nat prefers *me* – he told me so!"

"Oh, yeah, right," I'd said in a bored voice. "That must be why he told me not to leave him alone with you because you're too full-on!"

"You don't know what you're talking about—" Gemma began.

"No, I know *exactly* what's going on," I cut in. "This is all part of your pathetic attempt to pretend you're not like me at all and that just because we're twins, we don't have to look the same and act the same. Well, that's fine, you search for your own identity if you want to – but keep your hands off my boyfriend!"

Oh my God, it was the worst row we'd ever, *ever* had. We weren't speaking to each other *at all*. Not that Mum had noticed, she was still too busy trying to cope with the fall-out from the rest of our extended family who had just been told about the separation. Mum's parents, our gran and granddad who lived in France, were threatening to come over, and, quote, "*sort Mum and Dad out*", and Mum was really stressing. Dad was still looking tired and anxious, too, although he'd picked me up and brought me to training tonight.

And then there were my friends…

It was my turn. I stepped up to the ball and kicked it towards Georgie. We'd all been sending texts to each other since yesterday afternoon, but no one had really apologised or tried to sort anything out. I could tell from the texts that they were still a bit annoyed with me, and also very confused by my behaviour, but I didn't think I'd done anything wrong. Not *really*.

Frowning slightly, Georgie hit the ball back to me, but she scooped it up into the air, rather than sending it along the ground, so that my first touch had to be a volley. I hit the ball cleanly and it zoomed into the top left-hand corner of the net. It was a great shot, though I say so myself.

"You've still got it, Grace!" Jasmin yelled as everyone, including Ria, broke into spontaneous applause.

Georgie raised her eyebrows at me and I could read in her face what she was thinking. *How can football NOT be important to you any more, Grace?*

"We thought you might not come tonight," Georgie said bluntly to me as we headed back to the changing-room at the end of the session.

"Why not?" I asked, feeling defensive.

Georgie shrugged. "Well, we didn't know if Mr Lover Boy wanted to meet up with you instead."

"I'm not that shallow," I replied, glad that my

cheeks were already hot and red from running around!

"Did Nathan Edwards *know* you played for the Stars, Grace?" Lauren asked curiously as she opened the changing-room door.

I nodded, feeling a secret thrill at being able to talk openly about Nat. "I told him straightaway. We decided it was better not to mention it to anyone else because of the rivalry between the Stars and the Belles."

Georgie snorted loudly in disgust, but a look from Katy stopped her from saying anything. Meanwhile, Lauren was frowning as we all began stripping our kit off.

"So Jacintha only found out yesterday?"

"I guess so." I had no idea what Lauren was getting at.

"*How* did she find out?"

I paused in the act of pulling off my shorts. "I don't know," I admitted reluctantly. I hadn't really thought about it, to be honest, but now that Lauren had mentioned it, it was actually a bit of a mystery. "Maybe she saw me and Nat together somewhere."

"Or maybe *he* told her," Georgie observed, kicking off her boots.

Lauren nodded. "That's what I was thinking," she remarked.

Anger flared inside me. "Nat wouldn't do that," I snapped. "We agreed not to."

"Yeah, but he might not have been able to help himself," Georgie said, her voice full of scorn. "I've got three brothers. I know what boys are like. He might have been boasting to Jacintha about the fact that he's managed to pull a gorgeous girl who's one of the best strikers in the league—"

"You don't know Nat at all, so just shut up!" I yelled at her. I saw the girls glance meaningfully at each other, and it *really* got to me. Turning my back on them, biting my lip, I climbed quickly into my jeans and grabbed my bag. I didn't even bother to change out of my Springhill Stars shirt.

"Don't leave like this, Grace," Hannah said pleadingly as I went over to the door. "Georgie didn't mean it."

"I was just *saying*—" Georgie began, but stopped abruptly when Jasmin chucked a sock at her.

"Look, guys, just let it go, OK?" I sighed, pausing in the doorway. "It's bad enough fighting with Gemma about Nat. I don't want to be fighting with *you*, too."

"Why are you fighting with Gemma?" Katy asked curiously.

"She's been flirting non-stop with Nat and trying to steal him away from me," I muttered, feeling hurt and angry all over again. "She *says* he likes her best, but I know she's lying."

The girls were all exchanging looks again, and it was *totally* starting to get on my nerves.

"Why does Gemma think that?" Jasmin wanted to know.

"Did Nat tell her?" Georgie again.

I stared at her. "Of *course* not! He likes me best, he said so."

"Maybe he told Gemma the same thing?" Hannah suggested a bit timidly.

Anger flared up in me again. "Nat would never do *that*!" I retorted, and then I walked right out of the changing-room before I said something I might regret. I heard Katy call after me, "We'll see you at the park tomorrow afternoon, won't we, Grace?" But I didn't reply. We always met up in the park on Friday before a Saturday game, but right now I didn't want anything much to do with the others after all the things they'd said about Nat.

I couldn't get that stuff out of my head though, as

I wandered through the college to the car park where Dad was waiting. Could Nat *really* have told Jacintha about us? I wondered. Maybe it had just slipped out when he was off his guard. As for all that rubbish about Nat telling Gemma *and* me he liked each of us the best, that simply couldn't be true. Why would Nat do that?

I could almost hear Georgie's voice inside my head. *Because he enjoys having two girls fighting over him...*

Stop it, Grace, I told myself. This wasn't the greatest of preparations for a tough match against our biggest rivals. The Belles would have a big advantage over us on Saturday now that we were arguing and not getting along. OK, I admit I still didn't want to lose that game, even though a lot of my interest in football seemed to have vanished. It was probably because I wanted to impress Nat and annoy Jacintha!

I knew I should really go along to the Friday get-together and try to sort things out with the other girls. I wasn't going to listen to any bitchy comments about Nat, though. They didn't know him like I did, and they were just being horrible because they blamed him for taking my mind off football.

Anyway, like I said, I did *mean* to go to the park to meet the girls, I really did. But on Friday morning I got a call from Nat, asking if I could meet him at the leisure centre pool that afternoon. I was so *happy*! I couldn't go to the park – I had to grab this chance to see Nat. So after a bit of thought, I just texted Katy and asked her to tell the others. Georgie would be annoyed and they'd probably say all sorts of things about Nat, but I didn't care.

Nat and I had a really fun time together. He even held my hand when he walked me to my bus stop afterwards! But somehow...that stuff the girls had said about him *still* kept running through my head over and over again, even though I *knew* it wasn't true. I didn't like to ask Nat how Jacintha had found out about us, because it would have looked like I didn't trust him. As for Gemma, Nat didn't mention her *once*. So, you see? I just knew he liked me best!

"Where've *you* been?" Gemma asked suspiciously, when I bounced into the house, singing happily to myself. "I thought you were going to the park to meet the girls, but your hair's all wet."

"Er, I met Nat at the leisure centre," I said, this time determined not to lose my temper. Of course I was glad Nat preferred me, but I didn't want to hurt Gemma's feelings. We might not have been getting on very well, but she was still my twin sister.

Gemma frowned. "Did he say anything about us? Me and him?"

I shook my head. "No, why would he? I know you're friends, but—"

"Nat said he was going to tell you he only wants to be friends with you," Gemma broke in. "It's *me* he wants to go out with—"

"Oh, get real!" I groaned. "Why does he keep asking to see me then?"

"Why does he keep asking to see *me*?" Gemma shot back. "It's ridiculous the way you keep pestering him, Grace!"

"*Pestering!*" I almost choked on the word, I was so angry. "It's not me who keeps texting him and getting on his nerves!"

"Oh, so why did Nat call me earlier and ask me if I fancied meeting up over the weekend?" Gemma demanded.

"He's probably going to tell you to butt out and leave us alone!" I yelled, "*If* he called you at all – you probably called *him*!"

"Are you saying I'm a liar?" Gemma's face was white with fury.

"Look, just leave it, Gem, OK?" I snapped. "We're just arguing all the time at the moment, and I'm sick of it! No wonder I'm thinking about—"

I just about managed to stop myself from blurting out, *"No wonder I'm thinking about leaving with Dad!"* I had to remind myself that Gemma and Mum had no idea yet that I was thinking of moving in with Dad – and probably no idea either that Dad was considering moving right away from Melfield.

Gemma was frowning, looking puzzled, but I didn't give her a chance to ask any questions. I shot off upstairs, cursing my big mouth, but things were so *difficult* at the moment. Dad wasn't here, Mum was distracted, the girls hated me being mates with Nat, and Gemma hated me for being the one Nat liked best.

There was only one person I could rely on, and that was Nat himself.

Well, that's what I thought...

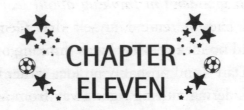

CHAPTER ELEVEN

I could not believe my *eyes*.

There I was, running onto the pitch with the rest of the Stars, feeling that maybe things were working themselves out, at last. Georgie, Hannah and the others had obviously decided that the match was more important than anything else, including me and Nat, and they'd all been OK with me since Dad and I had arrived at the college. It was a big relief, and to my surprise, I found I was actually starting to enjoy myself. The matches against the Belles always drew our biggest crowds of the season (if you can call people hanging around on touchlines a crowd!), and there was usually a great atmosphere.

"Right, let's forget about everything else and concentrate on this match," Georgie had declared, pulling on her goalie's gloves as we left the changing-room. "We're going to win this game, and we're going to win it in style! 5-0!"

We all cheered, even me, as we all piled into the corridor. The excitement was catching! At that moment the door of the away team changing-room opened, and the Belles started streaming out.

"Make way for the winners!" Lucy Grimshaw called as the two teams jostled each other good-naturedly on our way to the double doors at the end of the corridor. "We'll be six points clear again by lunchtime, Belles."

"That's what *you* think!" Jasmin squealed, looking *tiny* next to long-legged, broad-shouldered Lucy.

"We'll be level on points, you mean," Lauren added, "when we stuff you 3-0!"

"Our goal difference is better so we'd still be top, even if we lose 6-0 today," Sonia Ali said a trifle smugly.

Lucy whipped round to eyeball her sternly.

"We're not going to lose," she announced. "4-0 to the Belles!"

By this time we were outside and running onto our pitch. It was the perfect day for football, I thought, glancing up at the pale blue sky. The sun was out, but there was a slightly chilly autumn breeze, so we wouldn't get too hot. For the first time in ages, I was looking forward to the game. Maybe I'd been too quick to think I was growing up and away from football, I thought with a smile. I was *glad* that I was here today for the match with all my mates...

Then I saw them.

Gemma and Nat, strolling across the grass towards us. She had her arm through his, and they had their heads together, talking intently.

I felt like I'd been hit by a ten-ton truck. What were the two of them doing here – together? Gemma had been going to her dance class this morning, as usual, as far as I knew. Mum didn't usually work on Saturdays, but this morning she was covering a fitness class for an instructor who was on holiday, and I was *sure* I'd heard her say she'd drop Gemma off at the dance school on her way to the gym.

I couldn't take my eyes off Nat and Gemma as

they joined the other people standing around on the touchline. My mind was in a complete spin and my tummy was, too, so much so that I felt *sick*. What was going on?

I flicked an anxious glance at Dad who was standing on the opposite side of the pitch. He looked surprised when he noticed Gemma and Nat. They waved at Dad but made no attempt to join him.

"OK, this is *it*!" Georgie called us all together and we threw our arms around each other in a supportive huddle. Well, everyone else did. I just stood there staring at Gemma and Nat. Nat spotted me and waved cheerfully, but Gemma just looked stern and serious. I glared at her before Lauren yanked me over to join the rest of the team.

"Good luck, everyone," Georgie said urgently. "We *have* to believe we can do this – and we will!"

There was silence for a moment, and then, with a start, I realised that everyone was waiting for me, the captain, to say something.

"Yes, Georgie's right," I agreed lamely. "Let's just all do our best, and I'm sure we can win. Or get a draw, at least."

The girls looked a bit disappointed, but that was

all I could manage to say. I couldn't stop wondering what was going on with Nat and Gemma. The things Georgie, Hannah and the others had said about Nat were buzzing around my brain again, too. Had he *really* been stringing me and Gemma along all this time?

As the ref called to us to take our positions for kick-off, Jacintha Edwards ran past me.

"Nat seems to be very good friends with your sister, as well as with you, Grace!" she remarked with a grin, throwing a pointed glance at Gemma and Nat. "He's a bit of a lad, you know. He's got girls falling at his feet, and he *so* thinks he's all that!"

Lauren, Jasmin and Hannah were close by and heard what Jacintha said. I saw them exchange anxious glances. Meanwhile, I stood there rooted to the spot. I remembered, blushing, how quickly I'd fallen for Nat; how eagerly I'd dropped all my other plans to be with him whenever he called or texted me...

"GRACE!"

A shout from Lauren made me jump. We'd kicked off, and I hadn't even realised! The ball was spinning over to me and I lunged towards it, but couldn't stop it bouncing out of play.

"Sorry, Lauren," I called sheepishly.

Lauren frowned. "It wasn't even me who passed to you!" she exclaimed. "Didn't you see? It was Jasmin!"

"Sorry," I muttered again as Sonia Ali took the throw-in for the Belles. I had to get my act together right away, or I was going to be a useless waste of space for the Stars.

As you can tell, it was difficult to keep my mind on the game. Every single one of my passes, every one of my touches, seemed to be right off today. My mind was elsewhere as I went over and over in my head my meetings with Nat, our conversations, calls and texts. Had he just been enjoying mucking me and Gemma around and messing with our heads? Maybe he liked both of us and genuinely couldn't choose between us? Or maybe he just liked having two girls on the go, keeping us on tenterhooks and making us fight over him—

"GOAL!"

There was a roar from the whole of the Belles' team as Lucy Grimshaw collected the ball from Alex Lowrie on the edge of our penalty box and let fly with a thumping shot. Georgie's vision was slightly impeded by Katy and Jo-Jo in front of her, and the ball hit Katy on the leg and ricocheted into the goal.

One-nil. Only ten minutes gone, and the Belles were ahead.

Looking depressed, the Stars trudged back to our positions for kick-off as the Belles celebrated loudly. I knew that as captain, I ought to give the team some encouragement, but I just couldn't. All I could think about was Nat, and how stupid I'd been.

The Stars kicked off, and for the next ten minutes the action flowed up and down the pitch. It was end-to-end stuff so I had to concentrate, but it was difficult because I was trying to avoid going over to the side of the pitch where Gemma and Nat were standing. Stupid, I know, but it wasn't that hard to do because I was supposed to stay more or less central anyway.

Then the Stars had a great chance to equalise. Ruby got clear on the right and floated in a cross. I don't know if she was aiming for anyone in particular, but I could see the ball dropping down into the crowded penalty area right towards me. I just had to time my jump right…

In my anxiety, I timed it completely *wrong*. I leapt too soon and the ball grazed the top of my head and fell at Kellie Burns's feet. Looking relieved, she booted it away downfield.

"Idiot!" I groaned, really annoyed with myself.

"Don't worry, Grace," Jasmin said kindly, patting me on the back as she ran past. "You'll get a goal soon!"

Would I though, I wondered miserably. This was probably my worst game *ever*.

But things were about to turn even more disastrous.

I was hanging around in the middle of the field with one of the Belles' defenders while they attacked our goal. Most of them had gone forward, and Lucy Grimshaw was jostling Katy and Jo-Jo determinedly, anxious to take a shot as the ball bobbled around in the penalty area. Georgie waded in and somehow managed to belt the ball way up field. I tensed. The ball was flying towards me, and with only one defender and the goalie ahead of me, I had a chance to get forward. This was a Grace Kennedy speciality situation!

Then there was a gust of wind and the ball swerved slightly, heading for the side of the pitch where – you've guessed it – Nat and Gemma were standing. I stopped dead where I was.

"GRACE!" I heard Georgie's anguished cry right from the other end of the field. "What are you DOING!"

With no opposition from me, the Belles' defender had pounced on the ball. She instantly booted it back down towards our goal. All the Belles had come running out after Georgie's clearance, except for Sonia Ali who was lurking around the edge of our box. She was *just* on-side as she received the ball and brought it down. Side-stepping Debs and Jo-Jo, Sonia drove the ball hard and low into the net, past Georgie's outstretched hand.

"Y-e-e-e-s!" Lucy Grimshaw roared, rushing over to exchange high fives with Sonia.

The Stars were all frozen to the spot in disbelief. I swear none of us moved for five seconds, at least. Then, looking shell-shocked, Georgie finally managed to pick the ball out of the back of the net.

I couldn't see much as we kicked off again, because my eyes were swimming with tears I was *determined* not to let fall. Luckily, the ref blew for half-time just a few minutes later.

The Belles bounced over to their coach, chattering excitedly, on a complete high. In contrast, the Stars shuffled miserably over to Ria, who was looking anxious but trying to hide it.

"Sorry, guys," I muttered, hardly able to get the words out past the giant-sized lump in my throat. I knew that if Georgie or anyone else had a go at me, I'd just lose it and start bawling. "I'm not playing my best." God, the other girls must think I was *really* stupid to be so upset about Nat.

"We heard what Jacintha said to you." Lauren slid her arm around me. "Are you OK, Grace?"

"Is Nathan Edwards *really* going out with Gemma?" Jasmin's eyes were wide. "I thought he was *your* friend."

"So did I." I gulped. "But I think he's just been messing us about. Both of us."

"The cheeky little scumbag!" Georgie turned the full force of her fearsome glare on Nat, who was again deep in conversation with Gemma. "He deserves a good slap!"

"He's not worth it, Grace, *honestly*," Hannah said gently.

Katy didn't say anything, but she gave me a quick, comforting hug. I nearly started crying then and had to fight really hard to control myself. I hadn't expected the girls to be so kind to me. After all, it was *my* stupid mistake that had led to the second goal. But they seemed to care more about me and how I was feeling than the fact that we were 2-0 down. Even Georgie!

"OK, girls, let's just keep our heads and not panic," Ria said, handing out bottles of water. "We still have the second half to make a comeback. I want to see more team spirit out there. The Belles are pushing forward and leaving gaps at the back, and we should be exploiting that…"

As I was listening to Ria, hoping I could do better in the second half but dreading it, I saw Gemma coming across the pitch towards me. My heart lurched sickeningly.

"Grace…" Gemma whispered as Ria continued her team talk.

"What do *you* want?" I muttered awkwardly, moving aside from the others a little

Gemma hesitated. "I just wanted to say – sorry."

I stared at her in shock.

"I shouldn't have come here with Nat this morning," Gemma went on. "I can see we're putting you off."

I was silent, unsure how to react. I wondered if I should tell Gemma that I thought Nat was playing games with the two of us, but she'd probably bite my head off and not believe me, anyway.

"Look, Grace," Gemma was looking very worried. "You're not *really* thinking of going to live with Dad if he and Mum don't get back together, are you?"

I was completely wrong-footed. I'd expected Gemma to start boasting about how much Nat liked *her*, not me. This wasn't what I'd been anticipating at all.

"What—?" I had to clear my throat. "What do you mean, Gem? Where did you get *that* idea from?"

"I just guessed when we were arguing yesterday. We might not be getting on so well, but I'm still your twin." Gemma smiled ruefully. "I can still tell what you're thinking sometimes, Grace."

I sighed. "OK, then," I confessed. "It's been on my mind. But actually I think Dad's planning on moving back to Culverton—"

"*No!*" Gemma looked totally shocked. "You're not going with him, are you, Grace? You *can't!*"

"I don't know," I mumbled. "Maybe it'd be for the best..."

"No, it wouldn't," Gemma said quickly. "It's bad

enough Dad going, but I'd miss you like *crazy*."

"Would you?" I stared at her, a little surprised.

Gemma nodded. "I know I've been a bit of a pain the last few months, Grace." Her words came out in a rush. "It's just..." She heaved a huge sigh. "It's been kind of *hard* all these years, always being the quiet, shy one and watching you being all confident and outgoing. I desperately wanted to be *just* like you."

"You did?" I exclaimed. This was news to me.

"And then, when I finally started feeling more confident myself, I *didn't* want to be like you at all!" Gemma laughed, looking a little embarrassed as she ran a hand through her cropped hair. "I sort of resented being a twin, like I blamed you for holding me back all these years. I know it's stupid..."

"No, I can understand it," I told her, feeling my heart lift a little. Gemma and I hadn't talked like this for *ages*.

"And I just wanted to say..." Gemma looked a bit uncomfortable again. "It wasn't *my* idea to come to watch you play today. I know you probably won't believe me, but it was Nat's. He texted me right at the last minute when I was about to leave for my dance class."

"It's OK, I *do* believe you," I said quickly, wondering if I should say anything about my suspicions of Nat and his double-dealing. Would Gemma believe *me*, though? I had to give it a try. "I think Nat's quite enjoying having us fighting over him," I added cautiously.

Gemma stared at me, her eyes wide. "You know, I've been thinking exactly the same thing!" she declared. "It struck me this morning that he always seems to want to meet up with me when I've got something else arranged, like dance class, or seeing Maddy or my other mates."

"Me, too!" I agreed, remembering the agonies I'd gone through about missing training for swimming club, and then cancelling the usual Friday get-together with Hannah and the others yesterday. "I think he's been messing with our heads, Gem. Maybe he gets a buzz out of it?"

"You're right, I don't think Nathan Edwards is *quite* as cute as he seems," Gemma mused thoughtfully. "He wasn't very nice about your first-half performance just now, Grace, and we had a bit of a row about it…"

We both sneaked a look across the pitch at Nat. He was busy chatting to a pretty blonde girl, and hardly seemed to notice that Gemma had gone!

"You win some, you lose some, I guess," Gemma said, trying to smile at me although I could see she was gutted. She'd obviously liked Nat even more than I did. "Friends again?"

"Friends, definitely!"

And as I gave Gem a hug, she whispered in my ear, "Forget about Nat the Prat, and go get those Belles!"

I smiled as Gemma went over to join Dad, ignoring Nat. It was almost as if a mist had lifted around me and I could see clearly for the first time in *weeks*. Had I *ever* really lost interest in football, or had I been distracted because of the terrible situation with Mum and Dad? I wondered. Nat had become my escape from all that, so maybe that was why I'd allowed him to disrupt my life so much. What if I'd given up football completely to spend more time with Nat and *then* discovered that he just wasn't worth it? Georgie had asked me why wanting a boyfriend had to mean losing interest in football and treating my mates as second best. I'd just realised – IT DIDN'T! I'd just got things all the wrong way round. Like Hannah had said, boys would come and go (and Nat had very definitely just

194

GONE!), but that didn't mean I had to lose my mates *or* my football over it...

As the ref called us together for the second half, I spun round to face my dispirited-looking team-mates.

"Now you just listen to me," I said firmly, the light of battle in my eyes. "Yes, we're two down, but we're going out there to fight back, not to give in! You heard what Ria said: the Belles are pushing forward too hard and leaving gaps at the back, and we're going to take advantage of that. Do you hear me? We're going for the quick goal, and then we're on for the equaliser. Let's hit the Belles right between the eyes!"

CHAPTER TWELVE

Stunned silence!

Georgie was standing next to me, her mouth hanging open in surprise, so I slapped her briskly on the back.

"Come on, stop catching flies, Georgie Taylor, and let's get out there and strut our stuff!"

Georgie grinned hugely at me. "OK, captain!"

The Stars were buzzing now and really up for it. We ran back onto the pitch with our heads held high, and I could see that the Belles were surprised and slightly unnerved when they joined us. I wondered if they'd continue to push up or if they'd decided to drop back and defend in numbers. That would make it more difficult for us to get that vital quick goal, but the way I was feeling now, I could score a hat-trick against Brazil and win the World Cup on my own! Sure I was disappointed about Nat, but it was *such* a relief that Gemma and I were *really* talking again. That made up for everything. She and I could cope with our parents' divorce together, and support each other. I didn't need Nat any more.

It was the Belles' turn to kick-off the second half. But they didn't keep the ball longer than three seconds. Lauren was in there like a flash, sweeping the ball away from Sonia Ali and slotting a neat pass through to me. I latched onto the ball, turning Kellie Burns, and flicked it to Jasmin on my left. One-two and I had the ball back. and we were moving ever closer to the opposition's penalty area.

The Belles were looking a bit panicked. They had a fantastic defence, but they'd had it all their own way in the first half and I think the complete change in the Stars had spooked them a little! I side-footed the ball to Ruby who took a running shot. The ball slammed against the crossbar and the Belles' goalie gathered it firmly into her arms, looking relieved.

The goal kick sailed into the middle of the field, and Jasmin, Jo-Jo, Lauren, Hannah and Ruby were all waiting eagerly to fight for the ball. The looks on their faces almost made me laugh as I watched from slightly higher up the pitch. They were *so* determined. Jasmin was even gritting her teeth!

The Belles had no chance to get the ball. Ruby was in there, battling like a demon against Alex Lowrie, and even though Ruby tumbled over, she managed to get a toe to the ball and roll it over to Hannah. The break was on!

The Stars came sweeping down the field. Hannah to Ruby to Lauren to Jasmin. Kellie Burns wanted to spoil the party and tried to hassle Jasmin off the ball as she headed for the penalty area. But Jasmin just managed to off-load the ball to me before she could be robbed.

I didn't even have to look. I knew Lauren had dashed up alongside me into the penalty area and that she was in the best position of anyone to score. I tried to pass to her, but a Belles defender stuck her leg out and blocked the ball. The ball rebounded straight to Lauren though – result! Next moment Lauren's right foot had sent the ball snugly into the bottom corner of the net.

"YES!" I yelled.

God, you should have seen us – it was almost like we were winning 3-0, we were so excited! Yelling encouragement to each other, we charged back to the centre circle, eager to kick off again. Honestly, the Belles didn't know what had hit them! Jacintha was looking panicky, running around and telling them all to pull their socks up and concentrate.

"Wouldn't it be fab if we could get another goal really quickly?" Jasmin whispered longingly to me.

We nearly did! The Belles lost the ball to Katy near our penalty area and she made a winding run deep into the Belles' half before passing to Jasmin. Jasmin tried valiantly to set Hannah up with a shot, but the angle was too tight for Hannah and the ball zipped past the far post.

After that narrow escape, the Belles began to settle down again, unfortunately. They'd decided it was safer to pull back and defend, which was frustrating for us. Every time we got the ball and tried to go forward, there was a wall of red shirts confronting us. I was getting a bit anxious now. Time was ticking away.

There was a fierce battle for the ball going on in midfield. Lucy Grimshaw won it, at first, but her pass to Sonia Ali was rubbish, and Katy picked up the ball instead. She, Emily and Alicia passed it around between them for a few seconds as they struggled to get through the mass of Belles players blocking the middle of the field. Out of desperation, because it was her only option, Emily punted a long ball forward.

The pass was too long for anyone except me, and I was surrounded by three Belles defenders, including Jacintha Edwards.

When you think there's nothing you can do, go for the unexpected...

I trapped the ball and brought it down. One of the Belles defenders came at me, but I hooked the ball aside and went round her with ease. As I pelted forward, another one came at me and this time I nutmegged her – ha ha! – pushing the ball through her legs. I was now on the edge of the Belles' box. Just Jacintha left, now.

Jacintha and I squared up to each other. I turned away, shielding the ball from her and as she tried to hassle me from the left, I spun round to the right. I had to get my shot in fast, though, on the turn.

"GOAL!"

As the ball hit the net, I jumped up, punching the

air with excitement. Two-all! The crowd was applauding and the Stars were celebrating like we were winning 5-0! I was swamped by a sea of purple shirts as my thrilled team-mates rushed over to me.

"Grace, you're brilliant!" Hannah gasped, throwing her arms around me. I grinned. How *could* I have forgotten how much I enjoyed football when I was playing my best and I wasn't distracted by other stuff?

I couldn't help glancing over at Nat. But he was still chatting up the blonde girl – I don't think he'd even *seen* my goal! Well, I wasn't going to waste any more time on *him*.

"We'd better be quick if we're going to have a shot at winning this," Jasmin panted excitedly. "I don't think there's much time left."

The way the Stars were playing, we were on for the win, but Jasmin was right. Time was against us, and seven minutes later the ref blew for full-time. But if you could have seen the difference between the two teams at the final whistle – it was amazing! The Stars were still full of excitement at having come from two goals behind against the top team in the league, and we were really *up*. In complete contrast, the Belles looked disappointed and depressed, and Lucy, Sonia and Jacintha were arguing as they walked off the field.

"We're still only three points behind them," Georgie said gleefully, throwing her arm around my shoulders as we walked off the pitch. "If they'd beaten us, their lead would've been back to six points. And it looks like we've *really* messed with their heads!"

"Well done, girls – a great comeback!" Ria looked as thrilled as any of us as she rushed over. "Did you know, the Belles have won *every* game this season where they went ahead first? So you've done really well!"

"Thanks to Grace." Katy beamed at me and the rest of the team burst into spontaneous applause.

"Stop it, guys!" I laughed. "You're embarrassing me!"

It was then I noticed for the first time that Mum had arrived and was standing with Dad and Gemma. Immediately I ran over to them.

"Well done, Gracie!" Mum gave me a hug. "I got here just in time to see your goal."

"She was fab, wasn't she?" Gemma put in.

"That's my girl." Dad winked at me.

"Thanks, Dad." I hesitated, wondering if this

was a good moment to find out what his plans for the future were. Now that things were OK between me and Gemma and I'd got my football vibe back, I wasn't sure I wanted to leave Melfield and my mates at all. But I was still worried about Dad being on his own, so far away from us, making a new life for himself if he and Mum didn't sort things out. "Will you still be able to come and see me play every week though from now on, Dad?" I went on. "What if you decide to move a bit further away?"

Dad looked a little guilty. "Well, I've thought about that, I must admit. But actually I've very recently decided, whatever happens, to stay right here and rent a place in Melfield." He smiled at Gemma and me. "I'd miss my best girls too much if I moved away."

Gemma and I both breathed sighs of relief. Thank goodness Dad had changed his mind.

"Now, how about we go out for a celebration lunch?" Dad added. "My treat."

"Mum, too?" Gemma asked eagerly, linking arms with her.

Mum looked uncomfortable. "Gemma, I don't think—"

"Oh, *please*, Mum," I begged, slipping my arm through hers too. "Dad won't mind, will, you, Dad?"

"Of course not," Dad agreed, although he looked surprised and a little awkward, too. "Come on, Carly. For the girls?"

"Well, all right then." Mum laughed, a bit nervously. But Gemma and I were exchanging knowing glances. I guessed that she was secretly wondering, like me, if there was any chance of Mum and Dad getting back together! After all, they seemed to have got along OK since they'd told us they were planning on separating for a while. Maybe there was something Gemma and I could do to make a reunion happen...

"I'd better go and get changed," I said, seeing that Jasmin, Katy and the others were waiting patiently for me.

"Sorry, you lot." I ran over to them. "I'll have to be quick, Dad's taking us out to lunch."

"Your mum, too?" Jasmin asked curiously.

I nodded happily. "Maybe there's a chance they won't divorce after all," I said hopefully. "And good news – Gemma and I are best friends again."

"What about Nat?" Lauren wanted to know.

I grabbed a stray football lying on the pitch and kicked it right up into the air.

"Nat Edwards is exactly like that football," I said, straight-faced. "I've given him the boot!"

The other girls collapsed into giggles.

"If I get that stupid about a boy again and forget all about my football and my mates, you have my permission to give me a smack!" I said, joining in the laughter. "And I just wanted to say, thanks for not giving up on me when I was being a complete pain in the bum."

"That's what friends are for," Hannah replied, giving me a big hug.

"I know," I agreed gratefully, thankful that my life was partly back on track. Maybe there was hope for Mum and Dad, Gemma and I were friends again, my love of football was back, and I'd realised that I had FANTASTIC mates who were always there for me.

You know what? It's really not so bad being Grace Kennedy.

Ace, Grace!

About the Author

Narinder Dhami lives in Cambridge with her husband Robert and their three cats, but was originally born in Wolverhampton. Her dad came over from India in 1954, and met and married her mum, who is English. Narinder always wanted to write, but after university taught in London for ten years before becoming a writer. For the last thirteen years Narinder has been a full-time author. She has written over 100 children's books, as well as many short stories and articles for children's magazines. *Golden Girl Grace* is the fourth book in The Beautiful Game series.

Since her childhood, Narinder has been a huge football fan.

A message from the England Women's Captain

FAYE WHITE

With over 1.5 million playing the game, girls' and women's
football is now the number one sport for females in England.
I have played for Arsenal and England ladies since I was sixteen.
I grew up kicking a ball around – in the playground, at school, or in
my back garden. I was the only girl playing amongst boys, but I
never let that stop me, and I joined my first club at thirteen.
For me, playing football has always been about passion and
enjoyment. It's a great way to challenge myself, be active, gain
self-confidence, and learn about teamwork.
I have gone on to captain and play for England seventy times,
and achieved my dream of playing in a World Cup (China 2007).
I've won over twenty-five honours for Arsenal, including the
treble, and the Women's UEFA Cup.

Do you love football as much as me?

Then maybe, just maybe, you can follow in my shoes...
Practice, be passionate and strive for your dream. Enjoy!

Find out more about Faye and girls' football at...

www.faye-white.co.uk   www.thefa.com/womens
www.arsenal.com/ladies   www.fairgamemagazine.co.uk